SWITCHEF

A good old

"Jaimie McRae is hired to locate a missing woman. All the usual benchmarks are there—unhelpful cops, a hot secretary and girl Friday, and unexpected developments."
—*Pulp International*

"…something you might read out of a late 1930s pulp magazine."
—*Vintage Hardboiled Reads*

The author speaks…

"I like to write. I haven't any axe to grind, unless it's about people who think a story should fulfill some purpose other than entertainment. 'Didn't you enjoy it?' That should be the final criterion."

Robert Emmett McDowell Bibliography
(1914-1975)

As by Emmett McDowell

Mysteries
Switcheroo (Ace, 1954)
Stamped for Death (Ace, 1958)
Three for the Gallows (Ace, 1958; 3 novelettes)
Bloodline to Murder (Ace, 1960)
In at the Kill (Ace, 1960)

Science Fiction
Citadel of the Green Death (Armchair Fiction, 2019)
The Blue Venus, Sword of Fire, Black Silence & Moon of
   Treason (Planet Stories, 2021)

As by Robert Emmett McDowell

Fiction
Tidewater Sprig (Crown, 1961; historical/Kentucky)
Portrait of a Victim (Avalon, 1964; historical/Daniel Boone)
The Hound's Tooth (Morrow, 1965; mystery as by Robert
   McDowell)
The Sour Mash (unpublished mystery)

Non-Fiction
City of Conflict (1962)
Re-discovering Kentucky: A Guide for Modern-Day
   Explorers (1971)

Plays
Home is the Hunter (1964)

SWITCHEROO
Emmett McDowell

Black Gat Books • Eureka California

SWITCHEROO

Published by Black Gat Books
A division of Stark House Press
1315 H Street
Eureka, CA 95501, USA
griffinskye3@sbcglobal.net
www.starkhousepress.com

SWITCHEROO
Originally published and copyright © 1954 by Ace Books, Inc., New York. A magazine version was published as "The Tattooed Nude" by *Triple Detective Magazine* and copyright © 1953 by Robert E. McDowell.

Copyright © 2025 Stark House Press. All rights reserved under International and Pan-American Copyright Conventions.

ISBN: 979-8-88601-137-1

Text design by Mark Shepard, shepgraphics.com
Cover design by Jeff Vorzimmer, ¡caliente!design, Austin, Texas
Cover art by Victor Olson
Proofreading by Bill Kelly

PUBLISHER'S NOTE:
This is a work of fiction. Names, characters, places and incidents are either the products of the author's imagination or used fictionally, and any resemblance to actual persons, living or dead, events or locales, is entirely coincidental.
Without limiting the rights under copyright reserved above, no part of this publication may be reproduced, stored, or introduced into a retrieval system or transmitted in any form or by any means (electronic, mechanical, photocopying, recording or otherwise) without the prior written permission of both the copyright owner and the above publisher of the book.

First Stark House Press/Black Gat Edition: March 2025

CHAPTER 1

Jaimie MacRae was sitting in the back room of Gibbs & Stackpole, Inc., reading a murder mystery with exasperated fascination. Being a private detective himself, MacRae occasionally indulged in this form of mild self-torture.

In the story, the "private eye" was so busy climbing in and out of beds that he scarcely had time for the case. Moreover, the women were all young, beautiful and willing without exception. That was the part that stuck in his craw.

MacRae, who was approaching forty, couldn't remember that in his salad days the young women had been such pushovers. In fact, as he recalled it, they had defended their virtue pretty vigorously.

Admittedly, times were changing. For instance, there was that case in the papers where two women had raped a man at gunpoint. However, MacRae felt that such behavior was the exception rather than the rule.

With a snort of annoyance, he hurled the book across the room just as the door was cautiously opened. Miss Ives from the front office thrust her head inside.

Miss Ives never ventured all the way into the operatives' room. She was a slight young woman in horn-rim glasses, a brown tailored suit and sensible brown calf oxfords. Her brown hair was pulled back severely from her forehead, and her brown eyes regarded MacRae with intense disapproval.

"Mr. Dunn wants you," she said shortly. "It's a client."

MacRae heaved himself to his feet. He was a big man, built according to the general design of a heavyweight wrestler. His close-cropped sandy red hair was beginning to thin on top, and his pale blue eyes held about as much compassion as a barracuda's. Miss Ives flinched unconsciously beneath their bland scrutiny.

Ordinarily MacRae scarcely troubled to glance at her; but that damned book, despite its absurdity, had given him a vague feeling of inadequacy. Could he have been overlooking his opportunities?

Perhaps, he thought, he hadn't been able to see the trees because of the forest. Take Ives now. MacRae found himself seeing her for the first time as a young woman instead of part of the office furniture. He was surprised to discover that she wasn't at all bad looking.

"Ives," he said, "what're you doing tonight?"

Miss Ives was caught flat-footed by this frontal attack. Without actually saying so, she'd let it be known when she'd come to work at the agency that she didn't approve of detectives, or of mixing business with pleasure either. The other operatives—there were three of them—had been thoroughly intimidated by her icy efficiency.

"M-me?" she said, swallowing weakly.

MacRae leered down at her with alarming enthusiasm. "Sure. I've a couple passes to the fights tonight."

Miss Ives shrank away. "But the client—Mr. Dunn wants you in his office right—"

"I'll pick you up at eight-thirty, baby," said MacRae and gave her a smack on the rump that completed her route utterly. Miss Ives fled.

MacRae stared after her admiringly. "Holy mackerel!" he muttered in pleased surprise. Shaking his head, he went into Dunn's office.

SWITCHEROO

Isaac Dunn, manager of the Louisville branch of Gibbs & Stackpole, Inc., was a short fat man whose rimless glasses lent an evil glitter to his shrewd gray eyes. He said, with his usual economy of expression, "You know Mr. Warren."

MacRae admitted grudgingly that he did. However, he made no effort to shake hands with the client, who was sitting across the desk from Dunn.

Mr. Warren appeared more relieved than chagrined, as if he had been spared the necessity of embracing a performing bear. He was wearing a dark blue tropical worsted suit that almost camouflaged a small round paunch.

He smiled at MacRae and said placatingly, "I've a little job for you, Jaimie."

MacRae grunted, lowered himself into a chair. Any work that Amiel Warren wanted done would be smelly. The man was a criminal lawyer whose malodorous reputation was as well-known as his success. The only reason he hadn't been disbarred years before was his almost amazing instinct of self-preservation—this in a profession well known for its caution.

Isaac Dunn explained to MacRae in his precise voice, "It's the Hockmiller case. Mr. Warren wants us to try to locate Corinne Hockmiller."

"Why?" MacRae demanded.

"I'm representing Steve Hockmiller," the lawyer said.

"Little Steve?"

The lawyer nodded.

"What's his interest?"

Dunn interrupted impatiently. "Mr. Warren tells me that if Corinne dies or remarries, the money all goes to Little Steve. That's the way Big Steve left it. Corinne was to have the interest during her lifetime, but she couldn't touch the principal."

"I've explained to Steve," Warren hastened to add, "that the police are doing everything in their power to find her. But he isn't satisfied. Naturally, he's anxious for some positive information."

MacRae raised his eyebrows. He had been following the case in the newspapers with professional interest. Corinne Hockmiller, an attractive young widow with plenty of money, had vanished ten days ago from her apartment in the Tower Arms. Since her husband— Big Steve Hockmiller, a retired bootlegger who was reputed to have soaked away close to half a million dollars—had been killed last year, Corinne had lived alone. The maid, who came in once a week to clean, had reported her disappearance.

Apparently Corinne took only the clothes on her back. The remains of breakfast, growing mold, lay in the dinette. The bed was unmade. No money was drawn from the bank, and not one of Corrine's small, predominantly male circle of acquaintances could suggest where she might be. Corinne, they unanimously agreed, didn't discuss her personal affairs.

Her only known relatives were a sister in Cincinnati, who hadn't heard from her in three years, and Little Steve Hockmiller, her husband's nephew, whom she had forbidden to enter her apartment.

The will, however, MacRae decided, threw a somewhat sinister light on Corinne's affairs.

He said bluntly, "Little Steve wants proof that she's dead, is that it?"

"I didn't say so," the lawyer corrected him. "Of course, if her death could be established, it would eliminate a great deal of unnecessary delay."

"Um," said MacRae.

"Drop over and see Bridwell," Dunn told MacRae. "Get him to bring you up-to-date. And Steve Hockmiller wants to see you."

The lawyer added: "Steve has a lead he doesn't feel that he can give the police."

"What is it?" MacRae asked.

Warren shrugged. "I didn't ask him."

"Another thing, MacRae," Dunn advised his chief operative, "Hockmiller is our client. Please try to remember that."

MacRae got his hat from the back room, set it squarely on his head and started out.

Miss Ives, at her desk in the front office, was grimly slugging away at her typewriter. When she caught sight of MacRae, she stiffened and her cheeks warmed.

"Mister MacRae," she began firmly.

"Jaimie," he said, towering over her, an intimidating grin on his homely countenance. "Just call me Jaimie."

Miss Ives swallowed, took a steadying breath.

"I don't know what I could have done," she began weakly, "to give you the idea that I—I—That you would—"

She stopped in confusion. The glint in MacRae's eyes didn't add to her composure.

"Tell me tonight, baby," MacRae said before she could collect her wits. "I'm on my way over to City Hall now."

Miss Ives stared at the closing door with frantic despair.

In the lobby MacRae paused to examine himself approvingly in the mirror panel beside the newsstand. With his hat on, he didn't look a day over thirty, he decided, giving the double-breasted blue chalk-stripe coat a twitch and squaring his shoulders.

"Jaimie, my boy," he said complacently, "you may not have the profile of a Barrymore, but you're a fine virile figure of a man."

Major Bridwell, the chief of detectives, was bald, stocky, and abrupt, with eyes like a ferret's. He was ensconced behind a cluttered flat-top desk in a large room with three other desks and countless green file cabinets. He reared back in his chair as he surveyed MacRae with a complete lack of enthusiasm.

"Dunn phoned to tell me you were on your way over. I don't know what the hell you expect to find out that we can't, but you're welcome to go ahead. Here, you can have this." He tossed a police circular across his desk.

MacRae saw that it was a bulletin on the missing woman, which read:

ATTENTION ALL POLICE OFFICERS OF THE LOUISVILLE DIVISION OF POLICE

MISSING WOMAN—Corinne Agnes Hockmiller w/34, 5'2" 118 lbs., brown hair, gray eyes, light complexion, small build, scar lineal 3" on right side abdomen from appendectomy. Missing from Tower Arms Apartment 2332 James St., 7-3—about 9:00 PM
PHOTO ATTACHED

The glossy photograph stapled to the bottom of the bulletin showed a plump-faced brunette, whose eyes, despite retouching and a toothy smile, were uncomfortably hard and calculating.

MacRae folded the circular and put it in his breast pocket. He didn't like Major Bridwell and he didn't like to ask him for information. The major, in MacRae's estimation, was a thick-skulled, ex-football player who held his job by buttering up the right people while he rode the hell out of everybody under him.

MacRae could hear a loud speaker in the next room rasping out police calls, which poured in from all parts of the city. A teletype machine was noisily clicking off a message.

"Well," he asked finally, "what about Little Steve?"

Major Bridwell lit a cigarette, rocked back in his desk chair again and crossed his stubby legs.

"We haven't exactly overlooked him," he said sarcastically. "He's the only person who stands to gain anything by Corinne's death."

"Then you think she's dead?"

"Yeh."

"Any idea who might have killed her?"

"It's still a missing-persons case."

"What about her husband? Any line yet on who shot him?"

"That was a gang killing," said Bridwell sourly.

"I thought Big Steve had retired."

Bridwell stared at MacRae silently. At length he said, "From bootlegging, yes. But Big Steve Hockmiller controlled the handbooks here. When the election went against him last year, he began to slip." He shrugged.

MacRae was faintly surprised. He had known, of course, that Big Steve Hockmiller had been the Syndicate's number-one man in Louisville in the race-betting racket. But it hadn't occurred to him that anyone would have the temerity to buck the Syndicate. It could, though, explain a lot of things.

"Any connection between his death and Corinne's disappearance?"

"No," said Bridwell flatly. "It's been seven months since Hockmiller was killed. What connection could there be?" He obviously was rather sensitive on the subject. The handbooks were something of a thorn in the major's side.

MacRae, though, was not particularly disposed to spare Bridwell's feelings. "Big Steve was shot in the living room of his own house, wasn't he?" he said. "As I remember, somebody emptied a .38 into him. Where was Corinne at the time?"

"Out with some fellow by the name of Ward Bruton," the major replied coldly. "She and Big Steve hadn't been getting along. Naturally we check her alibi, but it held up."

"Who's this Ward Bruton?"

Major Bridwell stood up. "Listen, MacRae," he said, "I'm busy as hell. Why don't you talk to Sergeant Franck? He's on the case."

"Sure," said MacRae.

Major Bridwell told his secretary, a chunky young police sergeant, to find Franck. Franck, however, was over at court, and MacRae said he'd come back later.

Upon leaving the police department, MacRae ambled to the foot of Fourth Street, where his car was parked on the wharf to avoid parking fees. He felt mildly disappointed. So far the only woman in the case appeared to be Corinne herself, and she was missing.

In disgust, he got in his car, a battered dark blue Buick coupe of such an old vintage that it still had running boards. He headed east on River for Little Steve Hockmiller's place. Hell fire! He'd just started, he told himself reasonably. What did he expect?

The Venice was a huge, ornate structure, built to

resemble a Venetian palace with lots of fancy plaster molding, iron grill work, and colored glass. The façade was on the highway, while the back overhung the river whose brown surface flowed sluggishly past fifty feet below.

Built as a nightclub in the lush twenties, it had fallen on hard times, exchanging hands several times. It had been a private boat club for a while, then a beer joint, a dance hall. Eventually, it had passed into the hands of Little Steve Hockmiller, who had converted the building into a gambling casino and nightclub again.

MacRae pulled up in the parking lot at the side. There were a dozen or so cars lined up against the guard rail. The river was a mile wide here, and he could see the low green Indiana shore and an occasional white toy farmhouse. A sailboat was on the river, and a tug was pushing a row of sand and gravel barges.

He slid out from behind the wheel, walked around in front and through a hybrid Moorish-Italian entrance flanked by slim twisted pillars. The foyer had a tile floor, potted cactus, and a wide stairway circling up to a balcony. On the left was an arch with a lot of wrought-iron grill work, through which he could see the bar and a white-aproned bartender polishing glasses.

MacRae went in. He leaned an elbow on the bar and said, "Little Steve in? I'm from Gibbs & Stackpole. He's expecting me."

The bartender was a tall thin man in his late fifties. He looked at MacRae disinterestedly, then flicked on an inter-office comm beneath the mahogany bar. He said, "There's a dick here to see the boss. Yeh, private.

O.K." He looked at MacRae and said, "Upstairs to your left."

Little Steve's office was at the end of the hall. He was in shirt sleeves sitting behind an executive-type desk. A gaunt hollow-cheeked man with sunken blue eyes, he had a tight, bloodless, thin-lipped mouth. He didn't offer to shake hands and neither did MacRae.

"You've got a nice layout here," said MacRae approvingly and made himself comfortable in a red leather overstuffed chair.

Hockmiller sucked his teeth, eyeing MacRae with open dislike.

"Have you got anything yet?"

"Well, hardly. Warren said you had something for me."

"I want that woman found," said Hockmiller. Except for a few cousins of no consequence, he was the last of the notorious Hockmiller family. MacRae figured he probably got stomach ulcers seeing Corinne live like a duchess on the income from Big Steve's money.

"Dead or alive?" said MacRae.

Little Steve gave him a nasty look.

"I'm not saying it wouldn't be to my advantage if she turned up dead. But that's not why I sent for you."

"No?"

"No," said Little Steve. "I don't suppose you mind picking up a few extra bucks."

"That depends—"

"On what?"

MacRae couldn't think of anything offhand. "What's the deal?" he asked.

Little Steve leaned forward across the desk. "I want you to find out what Warren's up to. I think that damn shyster lawyer's pulling a fast one. Steve left half a million dollars tied up in a trust fund for that twist he married. A half million dollars! And Warren is the administrator. He's getting rich off the gravy from that job. But if Corinne dies or remarries, the money all comes to me and Warren is out in the cold, see. Warren ain't going to let that happen if he can help it. Maybe Corinne's dead and Warren's hid the body. If she ain't found, he'll have his fingers in that gravy for another seven years before she can be declared legally dead."

"Half a million iron men!" said MacRae in a tone of respect. At his present salary, he would have to work a hundred and twenty-five years to earn that much money. He found the thought depressing.

"I want you to go to Warren's house and nose around," Hockmiller went on. "He may be hiding Corinne for all I know. Maybe she's married again and he's trying to cover it up. She was hot for some guy by the name of Bruton. Ward Bruton. You look him up, too. He's a crap dealer out at Monroe Springs. She was running around with him before Steve was killed. And another thing, how do you handle your reports?"

"Dunn's the manager. We turn them in to him, and he passes them along to the client."

"Well, we're going to do this different. See. You report direct to me—and I'll tell you what to hand in. I don't want Warren to get suspicious. Just let him think he's getting the reports direct."

MacRae nodded, regarding Little Steve thoughtfully. What the chief of detectives had said had aroused his curiosity. He had assumed, heretofore, that Little Steve had stepped into his uncle's shoes as head of the gambling rackets in Louisville. He had been Big

Steve's chief lieutenant. He had all the contacts, knew the ins and outs of the business. Certainly he was the logical successor.

In fact, MacRae considered it quite likely that Little Steve had been the one who put the finger on his illustrious uncle in order to inherit the business. It was true that the police had been giving the bookies a rough time lately, but that had to be accepted as the natural result of the upset in the last election. In time, MacRae figured, the bookies would learn exactly whose palms to grease. The heat would go off and the gambling fraternity would once more slide along on an even keel.

However, if there actually was a rival contender for the job—somebody big enough, powerful enough, foolhardy enough to try to force out the Hockmillers and make the Syndicate like it—that gave an entirely different turn to the administration's present cleanup drive.

"Steve," he began, "do you suppose there's any connection between your uncle's death and Corinne's disappearance?"

"No," said Steve flatly. It didn't convince MacRae of anything but that it wasn't judicious to show any interest in the booking syndicate. "I've given you enough to start on. Get busy."

MacRae continued to regard Hockmiller with an amiable expression and didn't move.

"Didn't you say something about money?"

Little Steve frowned. "Ten dollars a day. You'll be drawing your regular salary from the agency. The ten will be extra."

MacRae looked disgusted.

He stood up. "I'm not sure I like your proposition.

SWITCHEROO

Not at that price."

"Fifteen dollars."

"Twenty-five," said MacRae.

Hockmiller got to his feet, his eyes mean, little bunches of muscle popping out at the corners of his mouth. "Who do you think you're trying to shake down, you chiseling, two-bit snoop?"

"Twenty," MacRae amended hastily.

"You damn robber!"

"From you," said MacRae, "that's a real compliment."

For a moment he thought Little Steve was going to crawl over the desk after him. However, Hockmiller managed to get control of himself. He nodded.

"O.K.," he said, sounding as if his throat was full of gravel. He pulled a wallet out of his pocket, counted out a fifty and four twenty-dollar bills and a ten, and pushed them reluctantly across the desk.

"I'd better get some action for this," he said in a voice that set MacRae's teeth on edge.

On his way out, MacRae stopped at the bar to wash the bad taste out of his mouth. He figured that refreshments, slightly altered, could be worked into his expense account. He had a bourbon and soda, a tongue sandwich, another bourbon and soda, a Swiss cheese sandwich on rye, a handful of ripe olives, and two hardboiled eggs.

A young woman in a tan Celanese suit wandered into the bar and seemed fascinated as she watched him stow the food away.

MacRae leered at her pleasantly. Her sun-streaked blonde hair was cut short and curly, and she was sporting a deep tan that made her eyes look startlingly blue by contrast. She bad a good figure, he noticed, although she was a little on the stringy side.

"Expense account," he said experimentally. "Have a drink."

The girl hesitated, smiled uncertainly. "I'll take a Tom Collins," she told the bartender.

MacRae was surprised like a man who gets a nibble when he doesn't believe there are any fish in the lake. Probably she got a rake-off on the drink, he figured.

"Do you read detective stories?" he asked suddenly.

She looked surprised. "Yes," she admitted. "Sometimes." The bartender set the Tom Collins down in front of her. "Thank you," she said to MacRae. She was eyeing him with growing interest. "What an odd approach."

"Why do you read 'em?" MacRae persisted.

"I don't know. Because they're exciting, I guess. Don't you like them, Mr.—"

"MacRae," he supplied. "Jaimie MacRae." Automatically he fished out an agency card and gave it to her.

"You're a detective!" the girl exclaimed, and widened her eyes at him. "My name's Betty Jean Coleman, Mr. MacRae. I've always wanted to meet a detective."

"Is that right? Why?"

"They—they do such exciting things. Like shadowing people, don't they? They're kind of different—"

"I never thought about it like that," said MacRae intrigued. "Yeh, I suppose you're right." He glanced at his watch, saw with annoyance that it was four o'clock and figured that he had time to take a quick look at Corinne's apartment before reporting in. "What's your telephone number?"

"But, I—I didn't mean—" she stammered in astonishment. "I don't—"

"That's O.K.," said MacRae unperturbed. "I'll find

SWITCHEROO 19

you, baby."

"But Mr. MacRae, I'm married!" she wailed in consternation.

"Fine," he said. "I prefer a woman with some experience." Then he went out, with Betty Jean Coleman staring after him in unconcealed dismay.

When MacRae drew up in front of the Tower Arms, he regarded the building with a troubled frown. It was a dirty, three-story, sprawling yellow brick building. Certainly not the type of place he would have expected a young woman to stay who enjoyed the income from half a million dollars.

He was even more surprised when, after flashing his deputy sheriff's badge, the manager let him into Corinne s third floor walk-up. MacRae was a man who could appreciate economy, but this seemed carrying it almost too far.

He shut the door in the manager's face and prowled through the four small rooms. There was a bath, a kitchen and breakfast nook, a bedroom and a living room. All were furnished in shoddy, mismatched furniture of uncertain vintage. The closet held a few clothes with labels from the cheaper shops. The chest of drawers was full of worn underthings: stockings, blouses—none of them expensive. There was a small radio that had cost possibly twenty-five dollars. There were only a couple of pairs of shoes.

Potatoes had begun to sprout in a bag in the kitchen, and the shelves held a scant stock of canned tomatoes, peas, and canned milk. There was half of a stale loaf of bread on the dinette table, an inexpensive toaster, and a stick of oleo.

"Holy mackerel!" he muttered. It just didn't make

sense.

He went over the apartment again with a patient thoroughness that overlooked no possibility. He even went out the back door onto a small balcony hanging over the alley and peered into the garbage can.

Returning to the kitchen, he stared at the chipped and stained sink, the unpainted wood table and chairs, the scuffed felt-base linoleum rug, and he wondered what the hell Corinne had done with all her money. Warren certainly should have some ideas since he had handled the estate. He decided to have a heart-to-heart talk with the lawyer first thing in the morning.

Out on the back porch, a board creaked. MacRae's eyes narrowed and he turned swiftly toward the door. Dirty lace curtains cut off his view. He was conscious suddenly of the suburban quiet of the streets below. It was hot and close in the kitchen, and there was a stale, dusty smell. The sound wasn't repeated.

He was about to turn away when a dark shape loomed against the curtain.

MacRae lunged forward like a bull. He seized the knob, jerked the door inward, grabbed at an arm and yanked.

There was a startled shriek, and the girl who was attached to the arm practically flew through the opening. Her eyes were so wide that the whites showed all around the iris, and her mouth was open to scream.

With admirable presence of mind, MacRae clapped his hand over her mouth, and kicked the door shut.

"You've got some explaining to do," he said harshly.

For answer, the girl bit him.

CHAPTER 2

MacRae, grunting in pain, indignantly snatched his hand away from the girl's mouth. But he didn't turn her loose.

"Go ahead," he said savagely. "Yell your damn head off. All it's going to get you is a ride downtown."

He could see the panicky look in her eyes begin to be replaced by an uneasiness. Her eyes were an odd tawny brown. Her dark brown hair was done up in curlers, and she didn't have on any make-up. She was wearing a wine-colored housecoat and slippers. MacRae figured she was about twenty-eight—maybe younger. He flashed his deputy sheriff's badge.

"Are you going to talk? Or must I pull you in?"

"Let me go," she said. "You almost jerked my arm out of its socket."

MacRae turned her loose. She flopped limply on one of the kitchen chairs, and the housecoat split apart above her knee, disclosing the inside of a tanned thigh.

She caught the direction of his intrigued stare and angrily snatched the robe together.

"I live next door," she told him. "I saw you snooping around the back porch, so I came over to see—"

"What's your name?"

"Franklin. Emily."

"Did you know Corinne Hockmiller?"

She nodded. "Of course. I told you I lived in the next apartment."

"Yeh," said MacRae. The pain where she'd bit him was subsiding and his annoyance was going with it. Emily Franklin, he noticed appreciatively, wasn't a bad-looking dish. The V-neckline gaped almost to her navel, revealing the inner swell of a pair of uncommonly attractive breasts. He was amazed. He must have been going around for years like a horse with blinders. With an air of desperation, she snatched the top of the housecoat together and buttoned it at the throat.

"Miss Franklin," he said, "how long have you known Corinne?"

"Ever since she moved here, but we weren't chummy. I just knew her to speak to. Why?"

"I'd like a look at your place."

Miss Franklin's eyes narrowed. "You don't think I'm hiding her?" she said indignantly. She jumped to her feet, switched to the door, and wrenched it open.

MacRae followed her along the back porch to the next apartment and inside to a small, stuffy kitchenette. The table had a red checkered cloth on it. Ivy was growing from a brass pot in the window. After the bleak, moldy emptiness of Corinne's apartment, this room was a pleasant relief.

He glanced in all the rooms, opened the closet, looked under the bed. He stuck his head in the bathroom and saw stockings drying on the towel rack. At length, he sat down on a wine-colored couch in the living room.

"Well," he said blandly, "she isn't here."

"What did you expect?" Emily Franklin crossed to a walnut secretary, got a cigarette and lit it angrily. But her odd yellow-brown eyes were puzzled.

"Have you talked to the police yet?"

"Of course. They questioned everybody in the apartment house. But I couldn't help them any." She blew smoke through her nostrils.

He asked, "Have you ever been arrested?"

Miss Franklin's jaw dropped. Then she put her hands on her hips and glared at him.

"No!"

"Married?"

"No!"

"Where do you work?"

"I'm the hostess at Arstark's."

Arstark's, MacRae knew, was a downtown grill too rich for his blood. He said, "What are your hours?"

"Ten to six."

"Why aren't you there now?"

"Because," she said indignantly, "this is Friday. This is my day off. But I don't see that this has anything to do with Corinne Hockmiller. I don't believe you're a detective at all!"

MacRae handed her an agency card. "The name's MacRae," he said. "Jaimie MacRae."

"Private detective!" the girl said. Her eyes narrowed. "You're the prowler who broke into Corinne's apartment."

"Prowler?" MacRae sat up suddenly. "When was that?"

"You know perfectly well when—"

"Quit stalling," he said harshly. "When did it happen?"

Miss Franklin swallowed, drew back slightly.

"Why—why, it was a couple of days before Corinne turned up missing," she said uneasily.

"Go on."

"Well," she said, "it was about two o'clock in the morning. I'd just come in and was getting ready for bed, when I heard this scream."

"What scream?"

"It was Corinne. She was yelling her head off. Then I heard her run out in the hall, and she began to pound on my door. I asked her what was the matter."

"Didn't you open the door?"

"Of course not!" said Miss Franklin indignantly. "How did I know what was going on out there? Corinne was crying: 'Please, please let me in. He's going to kill me!' I guess she must've waked up everybody in the building, because I could hear lots of voices in the hall. So I put on a robe and went out. The superintendent had called the police. Corinne was calmed down some by the time they got here. She told them it was a burglar who'd broken in the back door. But he'd been frightened off by her screams."

MacRae sat back, his tough, battered face expressionless. He glanced at his watch, saw that it was after six o'clock.

He leaned forward and to Miss Franklin's utter bewilderment, patted her fondly on the head.

"Thanks, kid," he said. "I've got to beat it now, but I want to talk to you again. I'll be seeing you."

From Miss Franklin's expression, it was difficult to tell whether she considered this a promise or a threat.

MacRae bought an evening paper on the way to pick up Miss Ives. He had showered, shaved, and changed to a gray gabardine single-breasted suit, for which he had paid fifty dollars in a fit of extravagance. He felt pretty smooth as he glanced at the headlines.

Corinne, he saw, had made the front page again. A fisherman had snagged a strand of brown hair below the dam, and the Inland Coast Guard Station had dispatched a boat to drag the river. There was a picture of the boat at work with the K & I bridge in the

SWITCHEROO

background.

MacRae thought it was considerable furor over a strand of unidentifiable brown hair. On page six there was another article that caught his eye. It was just a few sticks of type, saying that the vice squad had arrested three more handbook operators. Obviously, the pressure was still on.

Miss Ives lived in a neat, two-story white frame house, surrounded by a well-kept green lawn. MacRae pulled up in front, ambled across the grass to the door, and rang the bell. Almost immediately, it was opened by Miss Ives herself.

She was dressed in a green dotted Swiss dress through which he was aware of a trim figure. High-heeled shoes made her legs look longer, the calves more shapely. She'd put aside her glasses and done her hair in a looser style. MacRae was amazed by the transformation.

"Come in," she said. "Mr. Dunn said for you to call him the instant you arrived."

"How did he know I was coming out here?" he demanded, unpleasantly surprised.

"I told him. He tried to reach you at the police department, but you'd just left. And—and so I told him you would be here tonight—I—" she squared her shoulders. "Mr. MacRae," she said in a determined voice, "this has definitely—"

"Jaimie," he corrected, and thrust a florist box into her hand. "Where's the phone? I'd better see what's eating him."

"There." Miss Ives pointed helplessly with the box to a stand in the hall. "Is—is this for me?"

"Sure." He dialed the number.

"Gardenias," he heard her exclaim in a friendlier tone.

"They're lovely. But Mr. MacRae, you shouldn't—"

"Jaimie," he said.

"All right, Jaimie," she said with a touch of harshness. "Then quit calling me Ives! My name's Margaret. And another thing. I've been trying to tell you that—"

"Hello. Dunn? This is MacRae."

The receiver rattled metallically in MacRae's ear.

"Now, listen," MacRae said in a disgusted voice, "I'm taking Ives to the fights tonight. Put Walker on it."

The receiver rattled again. MacRae looked at his watch, said something under his breath. Then aloud: "Yeah, we'll have time, I reckon, if we hurry. O.K. O.K."

He hung up, stared at Miss Ives as if she were a total stranger.

"Get your hat," he said coldly.

Miss Ives swallowed and then went obediently into the living room.

"But, Margaret," an older woman's voice objected, "you said—"

A man chuckled, "Why do you think she got all dressed up, if—"

"Daddy!"

When she returned, her cheeks were flushed. She almost fled out the door and down the walk. They didn't say anything until they'd pulled away from the curb.

"Mr. MacRae," she began, then hastily corrected herself. "Jaimie, I don't want you to get the wrong idea. I mean about tonight. I tried to—"

MacRae said abruptly, "We've got to stop by Warren's house before the fights."

"You mean that lawyer?" said Miss Ives, disconcerted. "Why?"

"Dunn's a suspicious bird," MacRae growled. "He wasn't satisfied with Warren's explanation this morning, so he got busy as soon as Warren left the office. He found out that Warren's house in the country had been up for sale until Corinne's disappearance. Then Warren withdrew it from the market. He'd closed it up when his wife left him and was living in an apartment in town—"

"Why did his wife leave him?" Ives interrupted.

"What's that got to do with it?" MacRae snorted. "The point is, he sublet his apartment and moved back out to the country when Corinne disappeared. Another thing, you need servants to handle a place the size of Warren's, but he hasn't hired any."

Ives asked in a small voice, "Do you think he's hiding Corinne out there?"

MacRae shrugged. "Could be."

"Oh, dear," said Ives unhappily. "Why didn't I get a job in an insurance agency?"

"If anybody still thinks crime don't pay, they ought to see this," said MacRae as he turned into the curved private driveway that led back to Amiel Warren's place. The two storied colonial brick house was located in one of Louisville's most exclusive residential districts. It was set well back from the road, its manicured grounds surrounded by a low brick wall.

The house was dark except for a faint yellow light somewhere in back.

"Maybe he isn't home," Ives suggested hopefully.

"Good," said MacRae, "we'll be able to look over the place without interference." He stopped the coupe in the circle before the white pillared entrance and got out, his feet crunching in the gravel drive. There was a warm July smell in the air. The singing of katydids seemed to emphasize the stillness. The headlights of a car went past on the road in front of the house.

"Can't I wait here?" Ives asked nervously.

"Sure." He started for the front door.

He hadn't taken three steps when she said, "Wait a minute. I'm coming along." She scrambled out, her legs gleaming palely in the dusk.

The darkness was thicker on the porch. MacRae pressed the button. They could hear chimes pealing faintly from some place inside. After a while, MacRae rang again. He rang a third time and when no one answered, he tried the door. It was locked.

Ives breathed a sigh of relief. "We can't get in," she said. "Let's go back to town."

MacRae took her arm, steered her across the front of the house behind the cloister-like porch pillars. He had a small flashlight, which he directed on the casement windows. They were all securely locked and veiled by Venetian blinds.

"What are you going to do?" Ives asked fearfully.

"Case the joint," MacRae said out of the corner of his mouth. He was enjoying himself hugely. Particularly Ives' uneasiness.

She crowded closer. "Suppose Mr. Warren comes home?"

He paused at the edge of the house where a flagstone path dived into the shrubbery. The path, he decided, must lead around to the back where the light was casting a yellow rectangle on the lawn.

"Maybe you'd rather go back to the car?"

"No!"

"Well, stick close," he warned her, "and don't make any noise." He moved off along the path. Ives teetered on her high heels and clutched at his sleeve.

A screech owl suddenly whistled plaintively from the dark branches of a tree directly overhead. It was an eerie sound and so close that even MacRae gave a start. The girl gasped, whirled, charged straight into him. She planted a spike heel in his broken-down arch, wrapped her arms around him, apparently trying to run up him like a squirrel.

Caught off balance, MacRae sat down in a barberry bush with Ives sprawling on top of him. She didn't scream—she was too intent on getting away. A knee caught him in the side, an elbow jabbed his ear, and the barberry bush felt painfully like a pincushion. MacRae leaped to his feet.

"Goddamn it!" he burst out. "That's only a harmless little owl."

He got his hat and set it squarely on his head, brushed the seat of his pants, straightened his coat, and glared at the girl.

"An owl," said Ives with a gush of relief, and hung weakly to his arm. "Whew! I never heard one of the wretched little things before. Oh, why did Mr. Dunn want us to come out here anyway!"

It had grown quite dark. She was a pale blur beside him, and MacRae's ear was still ringing from her elbow.

"Not to wrestle," he said bitterly. Then in a somewhat less hostile voice, he added, "I told you Dunn thinks there's a chance that Warren may be hiding Corinne out here. Now for God's sake, try to keep quiet. We've already made enough racket to raise the dead." He steered her toward the rear of the house.

They came around the corner abreast and found themselves clear of the shrubbery. The house was built in the shape of an L, with a graveled car turn and the service entrance in back. The light was streaming from a ground floor window in the wing. It fanned across the graveled court, gleamed on the front fenders and hood of a dark sedan.

Miss Ives sucked in her breath. Even MacRae was disconcerted at sight of the car. It was a green four-door Mercury and appeared to be empty. He stood motionless a moment, saying nothing. Then he started for the lighted window. The girl kept as close to him as was possible.

The window was shoulder high and it was open, screened by copper wire. The Venetian blinds were rolled about half way up. He could see the wrong side of figured drapes. Not a breath of air stirred them. Careful not to touch the sill, he leaned forward and peered into the room.

It was a law library, he saw at a glance. The walls were lined with uniform yellow calf-bound volumes. There was a beautiful mahogany flat-top desk, mahogany filing cabinets, a mahogany table, several dark green leather chairs, a couch, a small fireplace.

And a dead man was lying on his face in the center of the Kirman rug!

There was no question but that he was dead, for the whole back of his head was gone.

Without MacRae being aware of it, Miss Ives had come up beside him and pressed her nose against the screen. Then she backed away, framed in the light pouring out the window. Her eyes and her mouth were wide open in a grimace of horror. Her first scream almost lifted MacRae's scalp right off his head. He lunged for her, clapped a hand over her mouth and cut another scream off in the middle.

"Shut up!" he said. "Shut up!"

She began to fight hysterically, twisting, squirming. He realized belatedly that his hand was over her nose as well as her mouth and that she was fighting panic-stricken for breath. He took his hand away from her face.

As he did so, he heard the whirr of a starter from around in front. The noise was as startling as a covey of quail bursting up unexpectedly from underfoot. Then the motor caught. It was his car. It must be his car!

He dropped Ives, who sat down limply on the ground, and ran for the path that led around the side of the house.

He didn't use his light. He was unarmed and didn't want to make a target of himself. He ran right over a clump of shrubbery, sprawled headlong, hitting on his left shoulder and the ear that Ives had jabbed with her elbow. He rolled to his feet, cursing out loud, and plunged on, but more carefully. He reached the front of the house just in time to see the tail light of his coupe recede down the curving drive, turn onto the highway and presently disappear altogether.

Swearing furiously under his breath, MacRae started back around the house. He ran smack into Ives and directed the flashlight to her face.

Her hat was cocked over one eye. Her skin looked bloodless beneath her make-up and there was a smudge of cross-hatching on her nose where she'd pressed it against the copper screening. The thought of being burdened with her in the present emergency didn't make him feel overjoyed. However, he couldn't blame her, he supposed. "They got away with the car," he explained acidly.

She said, "Oh," and teetered on her high heels.

He grabbed her hand and found it cold despite the warmth of the July night.

"That man back there," she said faintly. "Is it—was he Mr. Warren?"

"I think so." He scooped her up despite her feeble protests and carried her around the house to the back door. When he set her on her feet, her knees buckled and he had to catch her hastily under the arms. He could feel her shiver as if with a chill.

"I'm not going in there!" she protested.

He picked her up again like he would a recalcitrant child. The back door opened easily and his flashlight revealed a big modern kitchen, all white enamel, chromium, and dark red tile. He found the light switch, flicked it on, and deposited the girl on a chair.

"Hang your head between your knees," he told her.

She leaned over obediently, letting her head flop between her legs.

"Don't rupture a blood vessel," he advised her in a more sympathetic tone and started across the kitchen toward a swinging door.

"Where are you going?" she demanded quickly.

"Take a look around."

She was out of the chair and across the room before he had a chance to get through the door.

"You're not going to leave me here alone!"

He grinned at her suddenly. "O.K. Maggie. But don't touch anything."

The swinging door opened into a butler's pantry. Beyond the pantry was the dining room. He turned on lights as he went. There was a dark brown Chinese rug on the floor. The table was a modern reproduction of Chippendale as were the chairs and the sideboard.

The dining room gave on a hall and almost directly

across was the library, its door standing open, light pouring out. The house was absolutely still. Not even a board creaked.

A half-dozen steps carried him across the hall into the study where he squatted on his heels in order to peer at the dead man's profile.

"It's Amiel Warren all right," he grunted. As near as he could tell without disturbing the body, the lawyer had been shot twice in the face—one ugly hole slightly above his left eyebrow, the other just below the cheekbone. Both bullets had emerged from the back of his skull, carrying away most of it.

At sight of the body, Ives began to look sick again. She gulped and backed out into the hall.

MacRae straightened and silently stared down at the body. The dark coat was tight across the thick shoulders and hiked up in back. The knees were flexed, the feet shod in fine Scotch grain oxfords and argyle hose. There were no signs of a struggle. The air was warm and a little humid, and a subdued chorus of tree frogs and katydids rolled in through the open window.

MacRae found the phone in the hall, got the police, and described his car and gave the license number. Then he called Dunn at his home.

Dunn listened without comment, then told him to stay on it and hung up.

Ives said shakily, "Then you think it was the murderer who was in here while we were ringing the front bell?"

"Could be, but the cops are on their way. There's nothing to be afraid of now. I'm going to look over the house. Want to come along?"

"You couldn't pry me loose!" she said with a shiver.

It took them only a moment to tour the first floor. Ives approached each room with deep mistrust as if it might contain another body. However, the rooms were untenanted. The Venetian blinds were all closed, and there was a film of dust over most of the furniture.

The second floor was the same. Only the master bedroom showed any signs of occupancy: a tie was hung across the back of a chair; in an adjoining bath were a couple of damp towels, shaving brush and razor.

"Didn't you say Warren was divorced?" Ives asked.

"Yeh," said MacRae.

"But there's been a woman staying in this room," she said in a puzzled voice.

"How do you know?" MacRae shot her a quick glance.

"It's the air," she said doubtfully. "Don't you smell it? I think it's toilet water and scented powder. It just smells like a woman's room."

Using his handkerchief, MacRae opened the closet. It was full of men's clothes. Nowhere was there any sign of feminine occupancy.

"I don't care," Ives said. "There's been a woman staying here!" She bent suddenly over a fluted wastebasket beside the dressing table. "Look!" she said triumphantly and held out a tiny square of cardboard about as big as a postage stamp.

MacRae took it, saw that it was a price tag, the type pinned to a garment, and read:

> Currie's
> Dept. 10
> X-377
> $12.95

Currie's was an exclusive department store, catering largely to women. However, it also had a men's shop.

"It doesn't mean anything," he said, but he dropped the tag in his pocket.

From far away, the faint wail of a siren penetrated the closed room. Ives shivered. MacRae went to the window, but the leafy branches of trees reared a black wall around the house. He didn't move away, though, but continued to stare out into the darkness, gauging the approach of the prowl car by the ascending scream of the siren. In a moment, he detected another siren, its wail rising faintly in the distance.

He shook his head unhappily. Warren's death was a catastrophe. A hundred and forty dollars a week it was going to cost him; for there was no reason now for Little Steve to pay him extra.

CHAPTER 3

MacRae sat in Isaac Dunn's office with his hat on, his features blandly placid. He smoked and listened to Dunn and Little Steve Hockmiller, who were facing each other across the desk.

Dunn was saying, "You understand, Mr. Hockmiller, this killing throws a different light on the case. We don't handle murder investigations."

"I don't give a goddamn who gave it to Warren," Little Steve informed Dunn coldly. He was wearing an ill-fitting tan Palm Beach suit and a straw hat. He looked like a big, loose-jointed farmer. "All I want is a line on Corinne."

Dunn considered Steve Hockmiller's request. At length, he said, "We can't guarantee anything.

However, we'll keep after her."

"I want action," Steve said. "I want her body found."

MacRae leaned forward. "Why are you so sure she's dead?"

"What dame's going to run away from half a million bucks?" he demanded sarcastically.

"A good point," MacRae agreed. "By the way, where did Big Steve meet her?"

"She was Warren's secretary."

MacRae's pale, sandy eyebrows lifted slightly. "Where did she come from? How long had she been with Warren before she quit to marry Big Steve?"

Little Steve shrugged. "She was the reason that Warren's wife quit him, and a month after Corinne married my uncle she was running around with a stick man out at Monroe Springs."

"Bruton?"

"That's right."

"How did you find out about it?"

"I was having her tailed," Little Steve said. "I figured that when I got the goods on her, I'd show it to Steve. I had photographs, everything. I was about to spring it on him when somebody came along and plugged him."

"That was tough," said MacRae.

"Yeh," said Hockmiller, "wasn't it?" He stood up. "That's all I can give you."

"Any idea why your uncle was shot?"

"No."

"What about last night? Why would anybody want to kill Warren?"

"Why wouldn't they?" Hockmiller asked.

Dunn, who had been silent, said, "We'll keep you posted, Mr. Hockmiller."

Steve said, "Yeh. I'll be seeing you." But he was looking rather pointedly at MacRae when he said it.

When he had gone, MacRae took out his handkerchief and wiped his face. "An ugly character," he said unhappily.

Dunn regarded him several moments without speaking. MacRae wondered uncomfortably what was going on behind the manager's flat gray eyes.

"MacRae," he said at length, "whatever possessed you to take Miss Ives out to Warren's place last night?"

MacRae concealed his relief with an effort. For a moment he'd thought that Dunn might have got wind of his private agreement with Little Steve.

"I didn't know Warren had been shot," he said dryly.

"That's neither here nor there," Dunn said. "Miss Ives is not an operative. Have the police uncovered anything on Warren's murder?"

"No. I was talking to Emberger this morning. He's got the case."

"I see." Dunn dropped his eyes to the papers on his desk, dismissing him.

MacRae stood up and went out, closing the door quietly. In the outer office Miss Ives was sitting at her desk with her back to him. She was taking dictation from a cylinder.

He walked up silently behind her, jabbed a blunt forefinger in her ribs, said, "O.K., baby. You seen too much last night—"

Miss Ives let out a wild shriek, leaped straight out of her chair, which overturned with a crash.

"Startled you, huh?" MacRae said mildly.

She snatched off the earphone, and for a moment he thought she was going to hit him with it. Before she could make up her mind, though, the door to Dunn's office opened and the manager stuck his head out.

"MacRae," he said in a cold voice, "what are you doing now?"

"There was a mouse in her waste basket," said MacRae.

Dunn stared at them without saying anything, then withdrew his head and shut the door.

MacRae righted Ives' chair.

"Mouse!" she said bitterly. "I'm not afraid of mice."

"Have you got a bathing suit?" said MacRae.

"Yes, of course. Why?"

"Today's Saturday. You get the afternoon off and—"

"I'm going home to bed," she interrupted with considerable feeling. The police hadn't let them go until almost daylight and she looked hot and sleepy. Outside, the streets were already blistering and the office was like an oven.

"You can't sleep in this heat," he said imperturbably. "We'll drive out in the country. I know a lake where there's a nice little beach and a cool breeze, and you can lie on the sand and relax."

Miss Ives wiped her damp temples with a crumpled handkerchief, visibly weakening.

"I'll take you home at twelve so you can pick up your suit," said MacRae and started for the door.

"No corpses bobbing to the surface?" she asked timidly.

"Of course not."

"Where is it?"

"Monroe Springs," he said blandly. "It's a nice place. You'll like it."

MacRae walked over to Fourth Street and along it, staring in the show windows. Louisville was a one-

SWITCHEROO

street town. For the most part the better class stores, restaurants, and shows lined Fourth from the river south to Broadway. It was the heart of the big, sprawling, red-brick city on the south bank of the Ohio. Although it was only a little after ten o'clock, the sidewalks were thronged with people.

A blast of cold air met him at the entrance to Currie's Department Store. The damp chill of the air conditioning system gave him a clammy feeling. He stopped just inside the doors and let his eyes roam the sales floor. It was too early for there to be many customers. The clerks were busy dusting and arranging stock.

He didn't see anything of Miss Stevens, the store detective. He went over to the stationery department, called the operator on the house phone, and told her that he wanted to see Miss Stevens.

In about five minutes, she appeared on the escalator, gliding down from the second floor—a short, heavy-set woman in a dark blue linen suit that made her look even dumpier than she actually was.

"How's business?" asked MacRae.

"Picking up." It was a stock joke. MacRae didn't bother to laugh, and she regarded him with considerable distaste. Her eyes were like little shiny bits of blue glass. "The operator said you wanted to see me."

"Yeh. I'd like to find out if Amiel Warren had an account here."

"You working on that murder?"

He nodded.

"I didn't know your agency would take a murder case?"

"We don't," said MacRae. "Not ordinarily. The fact is,

we're on another case, but Warren was tied into it. I want to know if he bought anything here during the last couple of weeks."

Miss Stevens snorted, marched over to the glove department and dialed the credit office. A blonde salesgirl in a tight black dress was working a glove over a plastic hand. She had an exuberant bosom and the dress didn't minimize it. MacRae leaned on the counter and leered at her amiably.

The girl appeared somewhat startled. She gave him an uncertain smile. "May I help you?" she asked uncomfortably.

"I'm just looking," he said.

The girl colored.

Miss Stevens put the phone back on the hook, turned to MacRae.

"Warren had an account here," she told him, "but the books haven't been posted. They don't know whether he bought anything recently or not."

"What about the sales checks?"

She hesitated. "All right," she said impatiently, "we'll see."

They got off the elevator at the sixth floor. Miss Stevens put MacRae in an interviewing booth and disappeared into the general office. He lit a cigarette and relaxed as best he could in the little straight chair provided for customers. The clatter of typewriters, comptometers, and voices filled the air with a sound like that made by a noisy, hard-working bee swarm.

In a few minutes, the store detective returned with a sheaf of sales slips.

"Here," she said.

MacRae glanced through them eagerly: nylon pants, brassieres, dresses, stockings, an overnight bag, nightgowns, slips, cosmetics. They'd all been charged the same day—July 3rd—two days after Corinne Hockmiller had disappeared.

He looked at Miss Stevens, his face wooden.

"None of these charges have been signed for," he said.

"They were ordered over the phone."

"Then they must have been delivered."

She nodded.

"Who delivered them?"

Miss Stevens looked grimmer than ever. "Come on," she said, "we'll see if we can locate the driver."

MacRae followed her down to the first floor, and through a door with a sign over it which read:

NO ADMITTANCE
EMPLOYEES ONLY

He found himself in a noisy, confusion-filled place with a long bench against one wall where a dozen girls were wrapping parcels. A chute occupied the center of the room and there were bins around two of the other sides. The fourth side was open to the alley. Five delivery trucks were backed up to the loading platform.

Miss Stevens asked the man in charge which driver had the Mockingbird Valley run. The man yelled: "Hey, Nick," and a skinny fellow in a green uniform with "Currie's" sewn in yellow thread over the pocket of his tunic, left one of the trucks and came over. MacRae asked him if he remembered delivering some packages to Warren's place last week.

He thought a moment, said, "Yes, I remember it, because there were so many bundles."

"Who received them?" MacRae asked.

"Some woman."

"What did she look like?"

The driver's eyes lighted. "Boy! Boy!" he said. "Red haired—"

"What?" interrupted MacRae in a puzzled voice. Red hair didn't fit with his preconceived notion at all.

"She had red hair and—"

"Are you sure?"

"Sure, I'm sure."

MacRae took the police bulletin out of his breast pocket, showed the driver the photograph of Corinne. "Is that her?"

The driver studied it carefully.

"No," he said.

"Goddamn it!" MacRae burst out. "Are you positive?"

The driver nodded.

"O.K.," said MacRae resignedly. "Give me her description."

Sam Jenkins lived in the Grafton Apartments on Broadway below Third. He was a small, blond, wiry man with a big smile that showed lots of small white teeth. He let MacRae in, shook hands muscularly, then yawned and rubbed his short, wheat-colored hair with both hands. He was dressed in slippers, blue broadcloth pajamas and a blue robe.

He said good naturedly, "This is a hell of a time to come calling."

"It's almost noon," said MacRae.

"That's practically the crack of dawn," Sam said, and led MacRae into the living room.

It was about twenty feet wide by thirty feet long, with a grand piano in one corner and French doors opening onto a terrace. The woodwork was all white, the walls were tinted a sand color, and a sand-colored carpet covered the floor. There was a cabinet-model television set in another corner and a deep green couch in front of the fireplace. Draped over the piano, as if they'd been thrown there, were stockings, a dress and a slip. Sam gathered them up, collected a couple of highball glasses, said, "Make yourself comfortable," and left the room.

MacRae sat down on the couch. There was a big plate glass mirror above the fireplace and he could see the reflection of the gambler in the hall. He was opening a door and MacRae caught a glimpse of a bedroom and a woman in a pair of men's pajamas. Then the door shut, cutting off his view.

The woman had not been exactly beautiful, but there had been something oddly attractive about her. MacRae put her down as being in her thirties.

In a minute, the gambler returned, walking nervously on his toes like a boxer, which he had been. However, he'd been smart enough to quit the fight game before he'd been marked up. He had gone into bookmaking and was one of the three biggest layoff men in Louisville. MacRae had known him from his Golden Gloves days.

"Well, Jaimie," he said, sitting down and lighting a cigarette, "what can I do for you?"

"I'd like to know some things, Sam. For my own information."

Sam nodded, his eyes suddenly wary. "What are you working on?"

"The Hockmiller case."

Sam frowned. "I don't see how I can help, Jaimie. I knew Corinne, of course. She was a tramp. She's probably gone off with some man."

"Maybe," said MacRae. "But I think her disappearance has something to do with the Syndicate." He leaned forward, ground out his cigarette in an ashtray on a glass topped coffee table.

"It looks to me," he said, "like there's a plan afoot to kick out Big Steve's organization and take over the handbooks. That upset in politics. I reckon somebody figured it was a heaven-sent opportunity. But Big Steve was still too tough a nut to crack, so he was liquidated. Then the cops got orders to close up all the handbooks and keep them closed. What happens to Steve's organization? It goes to pieces."

Sam allowed a glint of worry to show in his eyes. He stood up, began to pace nervously back and forth in front of the fireplace.

"That's what's happening. It's easy enough to see," he said jerkily. "But I don't know who's in back of it. I'd give my right arm to know." He stopped in front of MacRae. "Listen," he said. "The really big layoff money from here is funneled to Cincinnati. You know that?"

MacRae nodded.

"I'll tell you something," he said. "They don't know who's engineering this. They're as puzzled as we are. But I don't see where Corinne fits in."

"Maybe she knew something."

"It's possible," Sam admitted without much conviction. "But Corinne wasn't too bright. Strictly a lightweight."

MacRae heaved himself to his feet. "What was Warren's connection?"

Sam gave him a sharp glance. "Didn't you know? Warren and Little Steve tried to take over the organization after Big Steve was killed. Warren was the fix."

MacRae raised his eyebrows. "But he didn't deliver, eh? And now he's dead. That doesn't look good for Little Steve, does it?"

Sam said dryly, "I imagine Steve has a satisfactory alibi."

MacRae grunted, stood up. "This isn't getting me any closer to Corinne. But thanks anyway, Sam." He started toward the door, paused. "By the way," he said, "what kind of louse is this Ward Bruton? I've got to run out to Monroe Springs this afternoon and have a chat with him. He and Corinne were pretty thick I understand."

The gambler allowed himself to look mildly concerned. "Another lightweight. But if I were you, Jaimie, I wouldn't do much snooping around Monroe Springs. Have your talk with Bruton, if you must, and clear out. Wheezer won't like you fooling around his place."

"Why not?"

"Just a tip, Jaimie. It's got nothing to do with Corinne."

"What about the Wheezer? Could he be trying to step into Big Steve's shoes?"

Sam shook his head. "He's in with Little Steve. We all are," he added ruefully. "But my God, I wish whoever is in back of this would show his hand. I wish I knew which way to jump."

The neon sign said: MONROE SPRINGS

"Here it is," said MacRae, and turned the car off the public highway onto an asphalt drive that cut through a grove of trees. The police had found his car abandoned not far from the Haymarket and he'd had to take a good deal of ribbing from them when he went to pick it up. MacRae didn't mind the kidding, but his gas tank was empty, and he had to pay the six-dollar fee for having his car hauled in. That hurt.

Miss Ives was regarding the woods rather dubiously. They had driven out from town and across the county line to Salt River where the resort was located. The countryside south of Louisville had grown progressively rougher, more hilly and lonely.

"There's the lake," said MacRae, pointing out the window. They could catch glimpses of it through the trees. It was the old bed of the river formed by a cutoff—actually a slough, several miles long, narrow, deep, and still. Dense undergrowth lined the steep banks. A canoe with three people in it was gliding across the brownish green surface. Then, as they came over a rise, they caught sight of the hotel itself.

There was something startling about coming on it that way. It was the last thing anyone would expect to find in the midst of that rough-wooded knob land. Miss Ives caught her breath.

In the first place, it was huge—a green painted, rambling two story frame building with a veranda across the front. Once it had been one of the most aristocratic spas of the Old South. During the season guests had come by steamboat and by private carriage from as far away as Georgia and Louisiana. It had boasted a hundred rooms, a glittering gambling casino, a huge ballroom. The grounds had been beautifully landscaped with terraces, formal gardens, and informal walks.

But all that had been before the Civil War. For a long time it had remained closed and boarded up. Then several years ago, it had been bought by a picturesque gentleman known as "Wheezer" Simpson. Wheezer had given the genteelly decayed spa a shot in the arm. He had installed crap tables and a blackjack layout in the old casino, hired an orchestra for the ballroom where a floor show, distinguished principally by its bawdiness, was put on twice nightly. But all these were part of its after-dark character.

During the day it presented a somewhat different appearance due largely to the lake. It appeared to be just a rowdy summer resort where couples could drink beer, and dance in their swimming suits to the music from a jukebox, where they could acquire a sun tan and ogle the girls in bikini bathing suits, and, perhaps, swim a little.

MacRae pulled up at the end of a row of glittering, high-priced cars, his battered old Buick looking like a junk collector's nag in a thoroughbred stable.

"Can we get something to eat here?" be asked the attendant, handing him a dollar, the admission fee.

"Sure," the man said, "through the lobby. The grill's in back."

Ives got her bag and purse out of the car, and they started for the entrance.

"This place gives me the willies," she said. MacRae didn't answer. He was curiously staring about, wondering where he could find Ward Bruton.

The lobby was a big, bare hall that ran straight through the building. A number of life-sized photographs of conspicuously unclothed young women advertised the floor show. A wide stair swept up to the second floor, and a huge prism chandelier hung from the ceiling.

The desk was on the left, but there was no one behind it. A card said: "Ring bell for attendant." They could hear a juke box playing somewhere and the murmur of voices.

"I reckon we go straight on through," MacRae said.

Ives suddenly clutched his arm as footsteps clattered overhead and started down the steps. They both stopped in the middle of the barn-like lobby, staring curiously at the curving stairway.

A red-haired girl descended into view. From below, she appeared tall and long-legged. She was wearing outrageously high, wedge-type sandals and a short, fingertip, terrycloth beach robe.

MacRae grinned appreciatively.

The red-haired girl grinned back. "If you're looking for the dressing rooms, they're in back," she said.

"Thanks," said MacRae.

She flashed him a parting grin and went through an archway on the right. She had a long, springy stride that imparted a slight swing to the beach robe.

"I think I'm going to like it here," said MacRae and glanced down at Ives. Her jaw was set.

"You look exactly like an ape with that silly grin on your face," she told him, and gave a startling imitation of his leer.

MacRae chuckled. He was beginning to feel that he had been in a rut for years.

They found the grill in a wing at the back of the hotel and had country ham with red gravy, French fries and coffee. The grill originally had been the kitchen of the old watering place. The fieldstone fireplace, complete with cranes, spits, iron pots, spiders, and ovens was high enough for a man to stand up in.

Men and women dressed in swimming suits, in brief shorts and briefer halters, in gay sport clothes sat about the rugged puncheon tables. MacRae could see the lake through the window. From the back, the reconverted hotel took on a startlingly different aspect. There were gaudy umbrella-shaded tables on the terrace. A crowd of bathers littered the tiny artificial beach, and he could see a small pier.

He and Ives separated to get into their suits. MacRae's shorts were of the gaudy, tropical print variety. He threw out his chest, sucked in his belly and ambled down to the beach, where he viewed the scenery appreciatively. If there was anything MacRae approved of wholeheartedly, it was the modern trend in bathing suits.

Ives came out, tucking a strand of hair under her black bathing cap. MacRae took one look at her and forgot all about the competition. She was wearing a one-piece black torso suit with a strapless top. Her legs were long and straight and there was enough meat on them so that they looked like legs and not stilts.

He was dumbfounded. Around the office Ives wore clothes that made her look like a stick.

"Holy mackerel!" he said with enormous enthusiasm.

"I didn't forget to fasten anything, did I?" she asked in a small voice and tugged at the ineffectual skirt of her suit.

"You better be careful," said MacRae. "You'll pop out the top."

She gave him a horrified glance.

MacRae chuckled lecherously and fell in beside her. Then his eyes lighted happily on the springboard. He used to be pretty good.

"Watch this," he told her and trotted out on the end of the board, testing its spring.

Satisfied, he drew back, took a careful preparation,

and tried a one-and-a-half layout. At the last instant, he had a dreadful flash that his timing wasn't what it used to be. Then he hit the water flat on his belly with a crack that sounded like a high-powered rifle. He came up gasping, feeling as if someone had sprayed his chest and stomach with gasoline and lit it.

He paddled weakly to the pier and pulled himself up out of the water. Ives was doubled up, laughing so hard that tears stood in her eyes.

MacRae glowered at her. "It wasn't that funny," he said bitterly.

Ives tried to stop laughing. "It was a lovely dive. A perfect one-and-a-half belly whopper. But doesn't that take a lot of stamina?"

She went off into another gale of laughter.

There were several other swimmers regarding him with broad grins. He stood up, stared at them coldly, and dived off the pier. He swam around until Ives slipped into the water, being careful not to get her head wet. They swam out to the float and back, and by that time he was beginning to get back his good spirits.

Ives was about twenty feet away, and he ducked under, swimming beneath the surface toward her. The water was a little murky but clear enough for him to make out her legs scissoring lazily. He reached out and pinched her calf as if a turtle had clamped down on it.

The legs exploded violently into action. A knee caught MacRae in the nose. He clawed his way to the surface, sputtering and choking.

To his disgust, it wasn't Ives at all, but an angry bald-headed man.

"Listen, buster," the man said, "go find some other

laddie to play with or I ram your teeth down your throat!"

MacRae was too shocked to take offense. He looked around frantically for Ives, discovered her sitting on the edge of the pier. She was holding her shins, rocking back and forth with laughter.

"Oh," she gasped as MacRae pulled himself dripping out of the water, "you should have heard that man holler. Oh, my side. It's simply splitting."

"I hope it's acute appendicitis," MacRae said bitterly.

Ives went off into another burst of laughter. "Please," she said weakly, "let's go over on the beach. I can't stand any more of this."

MacRae followed her rather grimly and sat down beside her as she stretched out full length. For a few minutes he contemplated the blazing July sunlight without enthusiasm.

"How about a beer, Maggie?"

She shook her head sleepily without opening her eyes. She was lying on her stomach with her face pillowed on her crooked arm.

He stood up and said, "I'll be back in a little while," and departed for the hotel.

MacRae dressed hastily and went on into the dim, cool lobby. There still wasn't anyone at the desk. He punched the bell viciously and in a minute footsteps approached. A young man in a yellow sport shirt and slacks came through a door behind the desk. He smiled mechanically at MacRae, said, "What is it, please."

"You've got a fellow here by the name of Bruton. Ward Bruton."

The smile went away from the young man's face. After a moment he said, "Yep."

"What room's he in?"

"You a friend of his?"

"I want to talk to him."

The young man hesitated. "He's probably asleep," he said finally.

"I'll wake him up," said MacRae, whose good humor had entirely evaporated.

The young man took another look at MacRae's expression, said hastily: "Room 87. That's back in the wing on the second floor. Turn right when you go up the stairs."

The upstairs hall was wide and uncarpeted, but MacRae's crepe-soled sport shoes made very little sound as he padded past closed doors that probably hadn't been opened in years. He found 87, rapped, but there was no answer. He put his ear to the door and listened. He thought he could hear someone moving around inside. He knocked again and the sounds stopped.

This was the quarter where the help was lodged, he guessed. A few electric bulbs dangled nakedly from the ceiling, but only one was turned on and it was several doors away.

"Open up!" he said, and rattled the knob. To his surprise, it turned easily in his hand and the door moved inward. He gave it a shove. It swung back and hit the wall with a bang.

Through the opening MacRae could see a bed and there was a man in blue-striped pajamas lying on it. He was propped on one elbow and he was holding an ugly black Colt automatic pointed straight at MacRae's navel.

"Pardon me!" said MacRae and stepped hastily sideways away from the doorway.

"Come back here!" the man called harshly.

"No, thank you," said MacRae and made several diminishing pats with his feet. He heard the springs squeak as the man sprang out of bed and rushed out into the hall.

MacRae clipped him behind the ear as he came through the doorway. He hit him so hard that the man's head bounced against the wood frame.

Wrenching the automatic from his limp hand, MacRae grabbed him by the collar and propelled him back into the bedroom. He shut the door and shoved the man back on the bed.

"What's the idea of pulling a gun on me, Bruton?" he demanded.

Bruton rubbed his cheekbone with a dazed, pained expression. He was a tall, lean, sallow man with brown eyes and dark brown tousled hair.

"Who are you and what the hell do you mean by breaking in here?"

MacRae ignored his question and let his eyes run around the room. It was big, high ceilinged, with an old-fashioned wardrobe, a chest of drawers and a rocking chair. Bruton's pants were hanging over the back of the chair, his shirt was draped on the mirror of the dresser. His shoes were under the edge of the bed.

MacRae's eyes suddenly narrowed. There were two pairs of shoes and one pair seemed to be balanced precariously on their toes. Before Bruton could sense his purpose, he stopped, reached under the bed. His hand fastened on a trim ankle, and he hauled a kicking, squealing girl out into the center of the room.

MacRae stared down at her blankly. It was the red-haired girl he'd seen in the lobby. Only she'd changed into a skirt and blouse.

She leaped to her feet and jerked down her skirt.

"Goddamn you!" she said. "Why don't you mind your own business!" And marched out of the room.

CHAPTER 4

As the door closed behind the redhead, MacRae removed the clip from the automatic and ejected the shell from the chamber. He tossed the empty gun on the bed, sat down in the rocking chair and studied Bruton speculatively.

A blue-black stubble shaded the gambler's lank jaws, and his long black hair was tousled from sleep, his pajamas wrinkled.

"I'm from Gibbs & Stockpole, Bruton. We're trying to find Corinne Hockmiller."

"A private dick," he said unpleasantly. "Who're you representing?"

"Steve Hockmiller."

The gambler's jaw dropped.

MacRae said, "Who was that girl hiding under your bed?"

"You've no right—"

"Oh, for Christ's sake," MacRae said in disgust, "you think I can't find out who she is?"

The gambler licked his lips.

"Mary Brown," he said reluctantly. "She's just a kid working here as a waitress."

"Waitress, eh? That ought to be easy to check. Now Bruton, what about Corinne?"

"What about her?"

"When did you see her last?"

Bruton looked just a little surprised and relieved as if he'd expected the questioning to take some other turn.

"The night before she disappeared," he said finally.

"Did there seem to be anything bothering her?"

"Yes," said Bruton. "Yes, there was. Somebody had broken into her apartment a couple of nights before and tried to kill her."

The platform rocker, on which MacRae was sitting, squeaked as he leaned forward suddenly.

"The hell you say! Why haven't you told this to the police?"

"Do I look crazy? She thought it was Little Steve. I'd never seen her so scared. She said she was going to see Warren the next day and that's the last anybody ever heard of her. That's the truth."

MacRae's face was impassive. Whether Bruton was telling the truth or not, it was only another blind alley, because Warren was dead.

He asked, "Who was shaking her down?"

"I don't know what you're talking about. Corinne never let me know if anybody was shaking her down." Bruton wet his lips again. "What makes you think she was being blackmailed?"

MacRae stared at him coldly.

"What was she doing with her money? She had the income from half a million bucks, but she certainly wasn't spending it on herself. What did you have on her, Bruton?"

"Nothing!" Bruton said, his voice rising excitedly. "I never saw a penny of her money. That's the God's truth!"

MacRae fixed the gambler with a cold, fishy eye. "You were sleeping with her. Don't tell me you don't know what she did with her money!"

"You're batty—"

MacRae cut him off. "Don't lie to me, Bruton. Little Steve was having you two watched. He's got the goods on you."

Bruton wiped the sweat off his face with his hand. "All right. What of it?"

"Are you still sticking to your story that you don't know what she did with her money?"

Bruton shrugged. "It doesn't make any difference now, I suppose. She's gone. That's why she never had any money, though. She was saving up for a stake. She was scared silly that Little Steve would have her bumped off. It was that damned will."

"Where did she go?"

"I don't know. She wouldn't tell me. She didn't even tell me when she was leaving. She just walked out. She made a complete break. Never even took any of her old clothes with her. Nothing they could trace her by. I think she might have gone to Mexico or South America, but it's just a guess."

MacRae scowled uncertainly.

"I think you're a damned liar," he told Bruton at last and pushed himself to his feet. "But I can't prove it. Not yet," he said and went out.

Bruton never opened his mouth.

MacRae shut the door firmly behind himself. There was a cold spot in the middle of his spine and it stayed with him until he turned the corner into the main body of the hotel.

He was more than a little puzzled about Ward Bruton. At first the stick man had been genuinely alarmed. MacRae would have been willing to stake his reputation, such as it was, on that. But once he'd learned that it was Corinne whom MacRae was after his alarm had evaporated. Bruton had been only too willing to answer questions about Corinne.

MacRae reached the lobby, but instead of returning directly to the beach, he decided to give the hotel a casual inspection. Bruton's attitude, coupled with Sam Jenkins' warning, suggested several not altogether fantastic possibilities.

On the south side of the old building opposite the wing, MacRae spotted the sloping doors of an outside cellar entrance. He stopped, lit a cigarette, and studied the doors thoughtfully. They were secured by a heavy padlock. The frame hotel had been built on a stone foundation about two feet high, in which narrow cellar windows were set at intervals. Each window was boarded up and covered with tar paper.

It struck him that someone had gone to considerable trouble to seal the hotel's basement. But why? What the hell was going on out here? The resort was situated conveniently close to Louisville but was across the county line beyond the reach of the authorities. There were no close neighbors to complain if things got a little rowdy.

However, MacRae knew that Wheezer had always been careful to avoid scandal in connection with Monroe Springs. The place was a gold mine. He kept the rowdiness within limits, ran honest games. Rough stuff was definitely out.

By George, but he'd like a peek at that cellar. He shook his head regretfully. He didn't think it advisable to try forcing entrance in broad daylight. But tonight—Ives would be a problem, though. Maybe he could persuade her to wait in the car? There was no real danger, but there might be considerable unpleasantness if he were caught.

He found Ives sound asleep on the sand with the late afternoon sunlight slanting across her. She had rolled over on her back with one arm flung across her eyes. Her shoulders, the upper part of her arms and breasts, and her thighs were turning pinkish.

"Wake up," he said.

She sat up quickly and wiped the perspiration out of her eyes. "How long have I been asleep?"

"Too long. Better get your clothes on or you're going to have a bad burn."

"I'm all sticky," she said. "Wait till I take a dip."

MacRae went over and sat down at one of the umbrella-shaded tables and watched her walk out on the pier. In spite of her slimness, she jiggled pleasantly here and there. He was still a little amazed and wondered how the devil he'd managed to work right there in the office with her for a year and a half and never tumble before.

She swam around a few minutes, then climbed out. The water had made her skin much redder.

"I'm beginning to prickle," she said plaintively.

"Let me see." He pressed a large, calloused thumb on her leg. When he took it away, it left a startlingly white print into which the blood quickly returned.

"What does that mean?" she asked.

"Sunburn. Turn around."

Her back was a deeper, angrier red. "You're burned, all right," he said with a low whistle. "Better get dressed," and gave her a parting whack on the seat of her bathing suit.

Ives gave a startled leap and marched off in indignation with MacRae leering after her.

SWITCHEROO

The early show was fairly mild. An M.C. came on and told a few smutty jokes, an aging blonde sang a couple of bawdy songs in a hoarse voice, took off her clothes indifferently and went off with her buttocks jouncing at each step.

Ives stared with a mixture of curiosity and disgust.

"I've never seen anything so repulsive," she said with conviction.

"I don't know," said MacRae argumentatively. "There was a peepshow in Yakima. You had to put your head through a hole—"

"I don't want to hear about it," she said emphatically.

MacRae noticed that her nose and cheekbones were red and whenever she shifted position she did so cautiously as if to keep her clothes from chafing her skin.

"Who do you think I saw out here while you were sleeping this afternoon?" he changed the subject.

Ives regarded him with sudden suspicion.

"Who?"

"Ward Bruton. He's running the crap game in the casino."

"Who's Ward Bruton?"

MacRae's expression was blandly innocent. "Corinne Hockmiller's boyfriend. You can imagine my surprise when I ran into him out here."

"Yes," said Ives gravely, "I can."

"He thinks Corinne's hiding out from Little Steve."

Ives didn't say anything. The ballroom was pretty well filled with couples. The evening crowd at Monroe Springs was louder, rowdier, and older. There was more drinking, and the orchestra had played incessantly.

"You know," went on MacRae. "He might be right.

Little Steve's desperate for money. It looks like he tried to knock her off once."

Ives shuddered. "That's awful. He's our client. Is that why he wants us to find her?"

"I don't know. But I'd like to take a look at the cellar of this hotel. I—"

Ives shot him a horrified glance. "Not tonight, Mr. MacRae!"

"Now, Maggie."

"No!" she said bitterly. "Take me home first. You almost had me fooled, but I ought've known you had some ulterior purpose when you brought me out here—"

"I sure did," said MacRae, and he leered at her wolfishly. Ives, who had been leered at by MacRae in earnest, was not impressed.

"You take me straight home," she said coldly. "You've got a one-track mind, and if I listen to you, I'll find myself creeping around in that horrible cellar."

He glanced at his watch. "But it's only ten o'clock."

"I don't care."

He shook his head sadly. "O.K.," he said.

"Is that a promise?"

"Yes."

Ives still seemed to be hesitating about something. At length she opened her purse and said dubiously, "Then I'll give you this." She handed him a triangular piece of cardboard. It was the lower diagonal half of a photograph. "I picked it up back by the incinerator—"

MacRae took the fragment. It was a five-by-seven studio photograph but the whole upper right-hand corner had been burned away. All that was left of the portrait was one ear and the shoulder of a young woman.

Across the bottom in a round immature hand was the inscription: "With all my love—Corinne."

"Where did you find this?" he asked gently.

"The incinerator."

"What were you doing there?"

"I woke up on the sand after you'd gone. So I went over to the grill looking for you. You weren't there, so I went back to the lake. But I took a different path and it went past a brick incinerator. That bit of picture had fallen out. I stooped over to look at it and I saw 'Corinne' written on it."

She regarded him defiantly. "I knew then why you'd brought me here. I wasn't going to show it to you until we were home—" She stopped, realizing that he was no longer listening.

He was staring somberly at the triangular bit of cardboard. Embossed inkless letters at the bottom read: Starre Studios.

He slid the fragment in an envelope and put the envelope in an inside pocket.

"Maggie," he said grimly, "I'm sorry, but I'm going to look this place over. You'd better wait in the car."

Her eyes grew round in alarm as he signaled a waiter for his check. It came to thirty-seven dollars.

MacRae glared down at it as if it were a live cobra. "Thirty-seven dollars!" he said in an ominous tone. "Who do you think you're kidding."

"You had dinners, you had drinks," the waiter said loudly, "you had entertainment."

Couples at the nearby tables began to stare. Surprisingly Ives said in an indignant voice, "Don't pay it!"

"I don't intend to," snapped MacRae. He looked at the waiter. "Get the manager."

The waiter opened his mouth to make some retort, got a good look at MacRae's expression, and changed his mind. "Yes, sir," he said hastily.

In a moment, he returned with a bald, middle-aged fat man in a tuxedo. The fat man broke into smiles at sight of MacRae, stuck out a thick-fingered hand.

"Well, well," he said heartily, "if it ain't Jaimie MacRae. How'd you like the show? Pretty hot, ain't it?"

"Hello, Wheezer," MacRae said grudgingly and introduced Ives.

The Wheezer acknowledged the introduction effusively.

"Classy," he said with embarrassing frankness and clouted MacRae on the shoulder. "How does a gorilla such as you rate a classy job like her? Lady," he said to Ives, "you got to watch this boy. He ain't no sportsman."

Ives looked overwhelmed.

"Don't flatter me," MacRae said sourly.

The Wheezer gave MacRae another friendly clout on the shoulder. "What's this I'm hearing about you boy?"

MacRae thrust the bill at him. "This damn bill," he began bitterly.

"That? That is nothing." Wheezer took the bill, tore it in half. "Today is on the house."

"Well, thanks," said MacRae.

"It's nothing," Wheezer said. "We're always glad to see you, boy. But not on business. No business. We like people to come for fun." He grinned amiably from MacRae to Ives as he escorted them into the lobby.

MacRae said, "I'm not interested in your setup here. I'm looking for—"

"Yes, yes," the Wheezer interrupted. "But believe me, boy, she ain't here. She ain't been here. No sir. She knows better than to show up here. I'd send her packing."

"Corinne?"

"Who else? Ain't that the one you're looking for?"

MacRae nodded.

"Well, she ain't here," Wheezer repeated and grinned at him benignly.

Ives put a hand on MacRae's arm. "Don't you understand," she said. "She ain't here."

"Well," said Wheezer admiringly, "a classy dame with brains yet."

"Mr. Wheezer," said Ives, "it's been a real pleasure to meet you. You're a man of discrimination."

"Not me," said Wheezer amiably, "I don't drink."

"That's men of distinction," said MacRae in disgust. "Well, if you say Corinne isn't here, that's good enough for me. I can take a hint. You don't need to hit me over the head with a club."

"I hope not," Wheezer said pleasantly. "I hope it ain't necessary, boy. But with you, I wonder—"

"What a funny little man," Ives said when Wheezer was gone.

MacRae gave her a sour look. "About as funny as a sawed-off shotgun. Come on. I'll put you in the car—" His jaws suddenly clicked together.

The two of them were alone in the foyer just outside the door to the ballroom. Directly across from them and beneath the stair was a passage which MacRae guessed led to the kitchen. Down this passage a short distance was another door standing open. From it came a grunting sound followed immediately by a man lugging a case of beer. The man turned away from them and started down the passage toward the kitchen, leaving the door open behind him.

MacRae's hand closed like a band of iron about Ives' arm. Without a word, he propelled her into the passage. Ives gave a startled gasp and marched along helplessly. A half-dozen steps brought them to the open door. Steps disappeared steeply downward into darkness.

"Just as I thought," MacRae muttered. "This leads to the cellar."

"You don't think I'm going down there!" Ives protested, pulling back. A dank smell, suggesting toadstools and moldering skeletons, rose out of the blackness.

They heard a door shut from the direction of the kitchen and the shuffle of approaching steps.

"Quick!" said MacRae, and he thrust Ives forcibly down the steps.

She went down, half falling, and was brought up with a teeth-shaking jar at the bottom. He yanked her unceremoniously to one side out of the faint shaft of light.

Before she could collect her wits, the door above them shut with a bang and there was the ominous sound of a lock being shot home. The blackness was so thick they could taste it.

"Oh, dear, we're locked in," Ives whispered in panic.

She gasped as the small pencil beam of MacRae's vest-pocket flashlight snapped on and swept around the cellar. It had an earth floor. Dusty bins lined the walls, which were stocked with big restaurant-sized cans of food. A stack of beer cases rose like blocks in one corner.

SWITCHEROO 65

"Must be the storeroom," MacRae said mildly. "This was too lucky a break to pass up. I'm sorry—"

Ives started up the stairs two at a time.

"Hey!" said MacRae, "you can't get out that way. Do you want the whole staff down on our ears?" He reached out quickly and grabbed her by the ankle.

Ives came to a sudden halt like a filly reaching the end of its tether.

"Now, listen," he said grimly. "There's another door on the other side of the hotel. An outside door. We can get out there without being noticed."

He grabbed her by the waist and lifted her down. Transferring his hold to her wrist, he directed his light on a rough plank door. He strode forward with the reluctant Ives in tow and pulled it open.

"There's nothing down here," he said.

"Then what are we doing here?" she demanded reasonably.

MacRae couldn't think of an answer and urged her across the threshold without too much difficulty; for her heels failed to dig in and she missed her grip on the door frame.

They found themselves in a long narrow room with diamond shaped bins lining the walls. A few empty kegs sat around in the midst of the litter.

"This used to be the wine cellar, I reckon," MacRae said. "They say old Colonel Monroe's buried here in the floor somewhere. He disappeared a little after the Civil War and there was talk that his nephew had killed him."

Cobwebs dangled from the ceiling, dust lay thick over everything, and the moldy smell was stronger.

"You mean he's buried here?" she asked.

"You might be standing on him."

She gasped and edged away. "Didn't they ever find him?"

"Nope. But the nephew never gained anything. People quit coming after the war. He went broke and hanged himself from that chandelier upstairs. You know," he went on, "Corinne could be buried down here. Who'd ever think to look for her in the cellar at Monroe Springs? Keep your eyes open for any signs of fresh dirt."

Ives shuddered. "If I ever get out of here," she said fervently, "I'll never speak to you again, Jaimie MacRae. Never!"

MacRae, though, was already moving toward a narrow corridor, from which they emerged into a great room beneath the main building. Huge poplar beams were supported by stone pillars. Junk was stacked everywhere; in places it rose as high as the ceiling. The room was like a rubble-filled chamber in Mammoth Cave—vast, echoing, black as pitch, festooned with cobwebs.

A big, brown rat, almost a foot long, suddenly scuttled across the path of light. Ives gave a half-stifled scream, put her hand to her mouth.

"Holy mackerel!" breathed MacRae. "Don't do that again!"

He began to pick his way through the litter, with Ives clinging desperately to his coattail. He reached the far wall and flashed his light about. There was an archway and a flight of stone steps leading upward to the sloping outside cellar doors above. Then his light found a roll of wire.

New wire. Beside it sat a case with a number of brand-new telephone headsets in it. There were a couple of big spools of the telephone cable sitting around.

MacRae stared at the equipment with narrowed eyes.

"I don't care what you've found," Ives said, "I'm going out." She went up the steps, pushed vainly at the doors overhead. "They're locked!" she called down in panic.

"Hey!" said MacRae. "Shut up!"

He ran up the steps and, crouching beside her, listened open-mouthed. He thought he heard footsteps on the gravel drive just outside. The footsteps were very close, and then he caught the mutter of voices.

His hand found Ives' face in the dark and slid over her mouth. "There's somebody headed this way." His hand tightened, stiffing her gasp. "Get down from here—"

At that moment, the footsteps reached the doors and stopped. Somebody began to fumble with the padlock.

The girl seemed paralyzed with fright. MacRae gave her a push. She blundered panic-stricken down the steps with MacRae breathing down her neck. In the darkness, he heard her high heels scrape the stone steps. Then she gave a half-smothered cry of alarm. It was followed by a bumping, scraping noise as she tumbled headlong. There was a thud and a crash.

"What the hell!" somebody ejaculated on the outside.

MacRae, charging down the steps on the girl's heels, tripped over some part of her anatomy, sprawled headlong, and brought up with a shock against a spool of telephone cable. He sat up dazedly.

"Maggie!" he said in a hoarse voice and began frantically to feel around for her.

Above him, the doors were thrown back with a crash.

A brilliant beam of light lanced down the cellar steps and caught him square in the eyes, blinding him.

"There he is!" a man's voice said excitedly.

MacRae, on his hands and knees with the light on his face, felt exactly like a mole who has just blundered out of his tunnel into broad daylight. He didn't move.

Footsteps thudded down the steps.

"Hey! Look at the dame!" another voice said.

"Shut the doors," the first voice snapped.

The second man retreated back up the steps and pulled the leaves shut overhead with a clatter.

"What the hell are they doing down here?" somebody growled, and MacRae realized that there were three men present. One of them pulled a string and a naked yellow light sprang on. The flashlight was switched off and MacRae could see again.

The first thing he saw was the muzzle of an ugly blue-black Luger staring him in the eye. It was held in the fist of a strikingly tall, emaciated man with a thin, hollow-cheeked face. He even topped MacRae's six feet two inches and must have weighed less than a hundred and sixty pounds. He had a big thin hooked nose, deep set gray eyes and a mouth like a steel trap. He was wearing a soft tan sport shirt and tan slacks. He said, "Frisk him, Joe."

The clerk in the yellow shirt edged around behind MacRae and ran nervous hands over him.

"He's clean, boss."

The third man was dressed in work clothes and had a belt of tools around slim hips. He looked like a lineman. He said, "I don't like this. What the hell are they doing here?"

MacRae pulled himself to his feet, moved over to Ives, and squatted on his heels beside the unconscious girl. She was sprawled on her face, one arm doubled under her, the other outflung. One knee was flexed and her skirt was twisted up diagonally across the back of her bare legs. He felt her pulse and to his relief, found it strong and regular. Running exploring fingers through the roots of her hair, he was unable to locate any bumps.

Then, to his astonishment, he saw an eyelid flicker involuntarily. She was possuming!

"All right," said the tall man. "Start talking."

MacRae could feel the sweat dampen the palms of his hands.

"Hey!" said the clerk, "it's that dick who was asking after Bruton!"

The tall man's eyes lit up with a pale, unpleasant glow. "Why," he said, "you're the shamus claims to work for Little Steve. Wheezer was telling me about you."

"That's right," said MacRae.

"Were you looking for Corinne down here?"

"Yeh," said MacRae.

The tall man began to grin. A long stride brought him within reach, and he suddenly slashed the barrel of the Luger across MacRae's face.

"I don't think so," he said.

MacRae blinked.

"Who're you working for?" the tall man said.

"Little Steve."

"You're a liar."

"O.K., I'm a liar," said MacRae.

"That's better," said the tall man. "Now, who are you working for?"

"I don't know," said MacRae. "You tell me."

The Luger slapped against his jaw again, and he

could feel the slight rip of his skin. A warm trickle ran down the side of his face. Blackness roared in his head. Then he got his eyes focused again.

"You want the truth," he said, "or you want me to make up a story to suit you."

"Keep on talking," said the tall man.

"I'm investigating the disappearance of Corinne Hockmiller for Little Steve," he said. "He sent me out here to talk to Bruton. He seemed to think Bruton might know something about her. You can check with Steve."

"I intend to," said the tall man.

"Well," said MacRae, "Bruton was pretty nervous when I talked to him. I figured he might know more than he was letting on. Then I noticed how the cellar was locked up and the windows sealed. It struck me he could be hiding her out down here. I thought I'd take a look."

The tall man shook his head.

"No," he said, "you're lying now. We've lots of empty rooms upstairs. Why would she hole up down here?"

"It was just a hunch."

The tall man hit him again. But this time MacRae let his head give with the blow, taking the punishment without a word, keeping his eyes fixed on his tormentor. Their pale, opaque blueness gave them a flat, shallow look as expressionless as the rest of his face.

The tall man shrugged thin shoulders.

"Then you've found something you weren't looking for, buster," he said.

The man who looked like a lineman gave a nervous start. "Take it easy!" he said uncomfortably. "If there's any rough stuff, I'm pulling out."

SWITCHEROO 71

"Do you think you're the only man who can install a switchboard, Cliff?" the tall man asked pointedly.

The lineman's weathered features turned gray. "No," he said hastily. "There's plenty of guys you could get. But the girl!"

"Who is she?" the tall man asked MacRae.

"Just a girl, I brought her along as a blind."

"Maybe we could get a little more out of you if we worked her over."

"For God's sake, don't hold out, Mister," the lineman said.

"Joe," the tall man told the clerk, "light up a cigarette. That'll wake her up."

The clerk ran his tongue around his teeth. With a sick look, he pulled a package of cigarettes from his pocket and lit one with a shaking hand. At the tall man's nod, he moved over to Ives and knelt beside her. The pungent smell of tobacco smoke filled MacRae's nostrils as the clerk nervously puffed at it until it glowed wickedly.

MacRae was standing flatfooted, hands dangling at his side. He didn't look at Ives. The lineman said, "Oh, God."

With the cigarette still dangling from his lips, the clerk grabbed Ives beneath her arms in order to roll her over.

Ives screamed at the top of her lungs, sure that the clerk had pressed the glowing coal on his cigarette against her skin.

The tall man jerked around as if he'd been jabbed with a bayonet. The Luger slid out of line with MacRae's belly. He promptly seized it by the barrel and twisted it out of the tall man's hand, kicking out viciously sideways at the stork-like legs. His heel smashed against the kneecap. There was an ugly brittle snapping sound and the tall man sat down, screaming in pain.

Ives had wrenched away and was scrambling desperately to her feet. The clerk snapped erect only to be met with the clubbed Luger squarely on top of his head. He fell down again. Bright red blood spilled from an inch-long tear in his scalp.

Cliff, the lineman, had recovered from his initial surprise and had yanked out a heavy pair of pliers. He rushed MacRae from the side, flailing wildly. MacRae flung up his arm to protect himself. The pliers hit his wrist and the Luger flew out of his hand.

He ducked another vicious swipe of the pliers, stepped inside, grabbed the lineman's belt, kicked his feet out from under him and slammed him to the ground. The lineman grunted, arms and legs thrashing wildly like a beetle on its back. MacRae kicked him behind the ear and he quieted instantly.

Ives was already halfway up the steps. She didn't even slow down for the doors, but threw them back with a crash and disappeared from MacRae's sight.

He scooped up the Luger and dashed after her, leaving the tall man writhing on the dirt floor. Miraculously MacRae's hat was still jammed down on his head.

Outside, he caught a shadowy glimpse of Ives who was already halfway to the car and running like a deer. Two men burst around the hotel drawn by the yelling. MacRae fired over their heads, and they skidded to a stop and ducked back around the corner.

He was wheezing like a wind-broken horse when he reached the coupe. Ives, he saw, had flung herself in behind the wheel and started the motor. She put the gearshift in reverse, shot back out of the line of cars, slammed it into first with a horrible clashing sound and roared past MacRae, almost running him down. He gave a spasmodic leap for the running board.

"Hey!" he yelled.

Ives didn't appear to hear him. With another horrible clash of gears, she rammed it straight into high, and they bounded past the startled attendant with MacRae clinging to the door frame by his fingertips.

At the highway, she slowed down to give him a chance to open the door and fall inside. The she tramped on the accelerator. They made the turn, wheels spitting gravel. Once they hit the pike, the coupe put its rear end down and scooted out like a frightened jack rabbit.

"Are—are they following us?" Ives gasped.

MacRae craned his neck around. "No." He fumbled out his handkerchief and mopped his face. "Who the hell do you think I am?" he demanded bitterly. "Tarzan?"

"I—I was scared."

He shook his head.

"With your instinct of self-preservation!" he said sourly. "What have you got to be afraid of?"

CHAPTER 5

From force of habit, MacRae woke at six the next morning. Then he remembered that it was Sunday and tried to go back to sleep. Habit won out. Irritably he heaved himself out of bed, showered and shaved, easing the razor around the cut in his cheek where the Luger's sight had torn the skin.

In the hotel restaurant, he ate hot cakes, sausage, orange juice and coffee, and read the Sunday paper. A man by the name of Sadler, he saw, had confessed to killing Corinne Hockmiller, but he hadn't been able to tell where he had hidden the body. In fact, all his information had been drawn obviously from the newspapers, and he had been committed to the City Hospital for observation.

There was even less about the murder of Amiel Warren. Police Chief Hendricks had released a statement that Warren's death was probably a gang killing, though the police were working along several lines of investigation.

MacRae snorted. To his way of thinking there was one item in particular that stuck out like a sore thumb. If that had been the murderer whom he and Ives had interrupted Friday night then how the devil had he got out to Warren's place? He had fled in MacRae's own car which meant that he had had no conveyance of his own. Professional killers didn't operate so haphazardly.

MacRae took his coffee cup back to the counter and had it refilled. He was beginning to feel almost human again.

In the feature section, he found a long article on legalizing the handbooks. An estimated sixty to a hundred million dollars were bet each year in unlicensed handbooks, the article claimed. If handbooks were legalized the city would net a tidy revenue. Moreover, a large percentage of this money was being drained out of town by the present syndicate.

Henry C. Coleman, Director of Public Safety, was quoted as saying that not only were the illegal handbooks a public waste but that they drew the criminal element around them. He pointed to the deaths of Big Steve Hockmiller and Amiel Warren, and while he didn't actually say that the killings had been connected with the gambling syndicate, it was clear enough by inference.

There was a cut of Coleman illustrating the article, revealing him as a big-jawed, clean shaven, pompous man in his early fifties. Under the picture in italics was: *"Safety Director Coleman says the handbooks must go!"*

He was a recent appointee, and MacRae thought that if he could get Coleman in a back room for five minutes, he could learn who was trying to take over the handbooks. A man like Coleman, though, who came from an old Louisville family and traveled with the country club set, couldn't be pushed around.

After breakfast, MacRae decided to drive out and see how Ives was getting along. She'd had a pretty bad fright last night, not to mention the sunburn. He had a pretty vivid recollection of her in that black strapless bathing suit. Ives was a good kid.

It was only a little after ten o'clock when he stopped the car in front of her house. The door was open and he knocked on the screen. He could hear a radio playing faintly, but nobody answered. He banged again. Then he stuck his head inside and called, "Anybody home?"

There was no reply. MacRae frowned. They could be at church, but he didn't think they would have gone off and left the house open and the radio on. His uneasiness gathered momentum. He went inside, banging the screen door.

"Hello!" he bellowed up the stairway.

"Wh-who is it?" a faint voice called down.

"Maggie!" he shouted irritably, "why don't you answer the door?"

"Is that you, Jaimie? I—I was afraid it was the police."

"Police?" He started up the steps. "What's happened?"

"Don't come up here!" she cried in panic, "I'm not dressed."

MacRae retreated to the hall. In a minute she descended the stairs, tying the belt of a peach-colored housecoat. She'd taken time to run a comb through her hair and apply lipstick. Her nose and her cheekbones were the color of a fresh cherry, and she looked feverish and uncomfortable.

"What's this about the police?" he demanded.

"It's against the law to break into a place like we did last night. I've been scared to death they'd report us."

MacRae began to chuckle. "They're not going to the police."

"Aren't they?"

"No, of course not."

"Well," she said dubiously, leading him into the living room, "I didn't know. I was afraid they'd take us to jail and it would be in the paper, and maybe we'd have to stand trial. Don't laugh! It wasn't funny to me!"

MacRae was looking around interestedly. The living room conveyed the feeling of being lived in. Crisp white lace curtains screened the windows. The walls and woodwork were tinted a pale blue. White crocheted doilies protected the arms and backs of the gray overstuffed suite. A nine-by-twelve wine-colored Wilton covered the floor.

"Where's the family?" he asked.

"Church. I didn't go because of the sunburn."

"Oh," said MacRae holding out a package, "I brought you something."

"You shouldn't have done that," said Ives. "What is it?" She broke the string eagerly and unwrapped a small jar. "Tannic acid jelly. What's it for?"

"Your sunburn."

"Oh," she regarded the jar dubiously. "But I've been using suntan lotion."

"Suntan lotion," MacRae said with contempt. "Let me see."

Ives obediently slipped the housecoat partially off one shoulder, revealing to MacRae that she had nothing on under it. "I couldn't bear anything against my skin," she confessed in some confusion.

"This is beginning to blister," said MacRae. "Go up and wash that damned stuff off and put on something that you won't mind getting stained."

Ives swallowed. "Wash it off," she protested, "but—"

"Don't waste time arguing," MacRae said curtly.

The burn obviously was painful enough that she was willing to try almost anything that might give her some relief. She went meekly out of the room.

MacRae got the telephone directory and sat down in a rocking chair beside the radio. He found a Mrs. Sylvia Warren listed, wrote down her address on an old envelope, and then went out in the hall and dialed.

He could hear the phone ring. Then a woman's voice said, "Hello?"

"Is this Mrs. Warren?" he asked.

"Yes."

"Mrs. Warren, I'm from Gibbs & Stackpole," MacRae told the lawyer's divorced wife. "We're trying to locate Corinne Hockmiller. Perhaps you can help us."

"I'm afraid I don't see how," the woman said. "I didn't

know her—"

"She worked in your husband's office."

"Yes, but that was several years ago."

"I know," said MacRae. "However, there's something come to light since your husband—uh—since Mr. Warren's death that I'd rather not discuss over the phone. Could I see you this afternoon?"

There was a silence from the other end of the wire. "Well," the woman's voice came faintly, "I'm going out this afternoon—"

"That's all right," said MacRae, "it'll only take a few minutes. What time?"

Again she hesitated. "I've an engagement at three," she said at length. "Two o'clock?"

"Fine."

"Who is this?" she asked quickly before he could hang up.

"MacRae," he said. "I'll see you at two."

He broke the connection, dialed police headquarters and asked for Sergeant Emberger, who was in charge of the Homicide Bureau and had the Warren case. He was informed that Emberger wasn't in and wasn't expected in.

He was just hanging up the phone when Ives returned. She had donned a pair of white shorts and a strapless halter, which emphasized the angry red of her shoulders, arms and legs.

"Hey! That's a bad burn," he said. "You're going to peel like a snake after this heals." He unscrewed the jar cap, releasing a ripe aroma.

Ives wrinkled her nose. "It smells horrible. Will it hurt?"

"No. Turn around."

"But I can put it on myself," she started to protest.

Encountering his bleak stare she subsided.

He scooped out a gob of the brownish jelly and smeared it liberally across her shoulders. The burn looked and no doubt felt a great deal worse than it actually was. Ives flinched. Then as he continued to smear the jelly over her inflamed back and arms and legs, an amazed expression flitted across her face.

"Why," she said, "it feels better already."

"Sure," MacRae grunted. The halter, he noticed, was tied in a bow knot. He loosened it, and before Ives realized what he was doing the halter dropped to the floor.

She gave a dismayed gasp.

"Hold still!" MacRae told her and put his foot on the halter as she made a frantic swipe at it.

"B-but—" she began, blushing scarlet and folding her arms in desperation. She would have taken to her heels but he clutched her firmly by the arm.

She gave a yelp of pain. "My sunburn!" she wailed reproachfully.

Startled, MacRae relaxed his grip. Ives snatched up the halter and hastily tied it back in place.

"Are you going to yell every time I lay a hand on you?" he demanded accusingly, untying the halter again.

She reached wildly for the ends. MacRae found the zipper on the side of her shorts. She had to drop the halter to grab at the shorts. "Jaimie, for heaven's sake!"

Suddenly she wrenched away and fled up the steps before he could stop her.

He stared after her in annoyance. Damnation! He'd probably scared the wits out of her.

As a matter of fact it took him a good twenty minutes to coax her back downstairs and then she came only after he'd threatened to come up after her. Also, she'd taken the precaution to don slacks and a shirt.

"I—I can't get over how much better I feel," she admitted in some confusion. "That stuff is wonderful. W-won't you stay for dinner?"

"Dinner?" MacRae decided in relief that he had been forgiven. "You sure it won't be too much trouble?"

"Of course not. And besides, Daddy's a detective story fan. He wants to meet you. Oh, here they are now," she added as a car pulled up in the drive beside the house. The sight of her parents seemed to bring her a certain amount of comfort.

Mr. Ives, Oliver as his wife called him, was a tall thin stooped man with an abundance of brown hair, twinkling brown eyes behind steel rimmed bifocals, and a dry way of speaking. He carved the roast expertly keeping MacRae's plate filled. He also insisted on guiding the conversation in rather gruesome channels for Sunday dinner.

"Tell me," he asked during dessert, "have you ever been on any murder cases?"

"Oliver, please!" his wife interrupted. "I'm sure Mr. MacRae's bored—"

"Not at all," said MacRae. "This is wonderful strawberry shortcake. My mother used to make it with piecrust, too."

But Mrs. Ives didn't take the hint. She was a slight prim woman of about fifty and was obviously terrified of their guest.

Oliver said, "I'm an accountant, Mr. MacRae. Murder mysteries make an excellent antidote."

"Well," said MacRae, "the last murder case I was on was back in 1940. I was on the force then. Detective sergeant. The Enschlaus case. Maybe you remember it?"

"No. We were in Nashville."

"Nobody even knew there'd been a murder," MacRae went on, "until a dog dragged a man's arm into a filling station out at Harrod's Creek."

Mrs. Ives made a faint gasping noise. She looked down at the scarlet berries in her plate and turned deathly white.

"Will you excuse me," she said, rising hastily. Before anyone could protest, she beat a retreat.

"I think I'd better go see if mother's all right," said Margaret and hurried out of the room looking rather pale around the gills herself.

MacRae, who had risen politely, glanced at his watch.

"You were saying—" said Mr. Ives, with a certain dreadful expectancy in his voice.

"It's twenty minutes to two," said MacRae, "and I've an engagement at two. I'll have to beat it."

"But look here," Mr. Ives protested. "You can't leave the dog gnawing on that arm."

"Oh, the manager took it away from him," said MacRae. He seized Mr. Ives' hand, pumped it twice, and dropped it. "I've enjoyed meeting you. Tell your wife how much I appreciated the meal. I'll see Maggie at the office tomorrow."

"Maggie?" Mr. Ives chuckled, repeated, "Maggie," as he escorted MacRae to the door.

MacRae was halfway down the steps when he happened to glance up and catch sight of a blue sedan as it started away from the curb about half a block down the street. It rolled slowly towards him. There were three men in the sedan and one of them was pointing at him.

He wheeled about and charged back up the steps like a fullback plunging off tackle. He caught Mr. Ives in the stomach with his shoulder and drove him through the door, where they both sprawled on the hall carpet.

Mr. Ives let out a pained, "Oof!" and his glasses went sailing across the floor.

At the same instant there were a couple of sharp raps against the side of the house, followed by half a dozen loud explosions, and something smashed into the stairway and sent splinters flying.

The firing stopped almost instantly as the sedan departed on down the street with a roar of acceleration.

MacRae picked himself up off the floor and put an eye cautiously around the edge of the door. The blue sedan, tires complaining, skidded around a corner and out of sight.

"Daddy! Daddy!" he heard Margaret calling in a frightened voice. "What happened?" Without waiting for an answer, she came clattering down the steps.

MacRae helped the older man to his feet. He was gasping for breath, for MacRae's shoulder had punched all the air out of him.

The ambush had left MacRae as unsettled as a cat whose tail has been stepped on. "There's nobody hurt," he told Margaret curtly. "Your old man just had the wind knocked out of him. That's all."

He brushed off Mr. Ives apologetically and set the glasses back on the bridge of his nose.

From the top of the stairs Mrs. Ives called, "Oliver! That sounded like a gun!"

"Was a gun," wheezed Oliver, getting his breath back. "Gangsters! Drove past the house and opened up on

Margaret's young man. Bullets came right through the screen. Look at that."

A slug had chipped the tread of the fourth step, glanced off, and buried itself in the riser.

MacRae said uncomfortably. "It can be fixed—"

"Fixed!" Mr. Ives took off his glasses and polished them excitedly. "That's going to be left exactly as it is. Right in broad daylight! Are you going after them, MacRae?"

"Hell no!" said MacRae indignantly.

"But—but who were they?" Margaret asked in a weak voice.

MacRae shook his head. "I don't know. They must've tailed me here." He got out his handkerchief, wiped his hands and face, and looked out the door nervously.

The sidewalk and street, shaded by young pin oaks, were deserted. If the neighbors had heard the gunfire, they must have concluded that it was a car backfiring; for the Sunday afternoon calm was unbroken.

"I'm going to call the police!" Margaret said in a determined voice.

"What'll you tell them?"

"Why—why—" Her determination visibly deserted her. "It was because of last night, wasn't it?"

"I wouldn't be surprised."

"But Jaimie," she wailed. "They'll come back!"

"I don't think so. They're after me."

Mr. Ives said, "You read about such things in the paper. But by heaven, they never seem real. Not until you actually see it with your own eyes."

His wife came down the steps like a mother hen whose chicks are threatened.

"Margaret," she said, "what's this about last night?"

MacRae squinted at her apprehensively. Little as

he looked forward to exposing himself in the open, he preferred it to facing an aroused Mrs. Ives. He said, "I've got to hurry. Good-by, folks," and ducked out.

Crossing the lawn he felt naked as a snail without its shell. But he reached his car without anyone popping out on him from behind a tree. He squeezed himself in behind the wheel and after a moment drove slowly off.

Sylvia Warren, the lawyer's ex-wife, lived in Oak Hill Manor—a modern development covering thirty or forty acres. The detached, two-story red brick apartment houses built in Federal style, were spaced graciously along winding asphalt drives and were surrounded by green lawn and shrubbery. The area was as confusing as a labyrinth, and MacRae drove around in exasperation for fifteen minutes before he located the right building.

He heaved himself out from behind the wheel and went up the walk skirting a tricycle, a wagon, two dolls, and a scooter. He was half an hour late as he rang the bell.

A woman of about thirty-five, in a dressy chartreuse afternoon frock opened the door about a foot and stared at him suspiciously through the gap. Her blonde hair was cut very sleekly in the latest style. Eye makeup emphasized dark blue eyes.

MacRae took off his hat. The woman looked puzzlingly familiar. "Sorry I'm late, Mrs. Warren. I'm MacRae from Gibbs & Stockpole."

"Oh, yes," she said unenthusiastically, and opened the door the rest of the way. "Come in."

The room was larger than he'd expected and furnished in a striking decor: monk's cloth draw drapes

SWITCHEROO

at the window, oversize armless couch and chairs upholstered in a heavy green ribbed material. MacRae's feet sank in a sand-colored Wilton rug. The room, he suspected, was typical of Mrs. Warren. She was essentially a plain woman smart enough to dramatize her good points.

"Won't you sit down?" she said, regarding him stonily. MacRae lowered himself into an upholstered chair and put his hat on his knees. He kept staring at her, then after a moment he remembered where he'd seen her. She was the woman he had glimpsed in Sam Jenkins' apartment. "Mrs. Warren—" he began.

"You said over the phone," she cut him off, "that something had come up about Warren's death. I don't see how that could possibly affect me. We've been divorced over a year. I wish you'd explain yourself. I've only a few minutes, If you'll just tell me what you meant—"

"Sure," said MacRae. "You're going to be dragged into this mess whether you like it or not. I'm sorry, Mrs. Warren."

"I thought you were investigating Corinne's disappearance?" she said sharply.

"That's right, but Warren was involved. When you divorced him, what arrangements were made for your support?"

"It was a cash settlement," she said, frowning doubtfully. "But I still don't see how—"

"You sued him for the divorce?"

"Yes, of course. It's all down in the records. He didn't contest it—"

"Exactly!" said MacRae. "Why didn't he? You took him for a good round sum, didn't you?"

She glared at MacRae with open dislike. "He didn't

contest it because it would have been useless. I had proof that he had been having an affair with some girl at his office."

"Corinne Hockmiller?"

"She wasn't Corinne Hockmiller then. Her name was Stevens."

"How long after that was it that Corinne married Hockmiller?"

"I don't know. Pretty soon."

"Then she must've been going with Big Steve at the time of your divorce."

Mrs. Warren sat back and regarded MacRae coldly. "Exactly what are you driving at?"

"You didn't sue Warren for divorce until after he and Corinne had broken up and she was engaged to Hockmiller. Why did you wait, Mrs. Warren?"

"You are an unpleasant man, aren't you?" she said. "But as it happened, Corinne and my husband did not break up—even after she married Hockmiller."

MacRae raised his sandy eyebrows.

"How did you find that out?"

"I—" she started and stopped. "You're just out here to fish for information. I'm in a hurry, Mr. MacRae—"

"Did you know the Hockmillers?"

She said, "Yes, naturally. They were clients of my husband."

MacRae hunched forward.

"How did you get the goods on Warren?"

"I hired a detective."

"Who?"

"Youngblood. I got his name out of the classified phone directory."

"What kind of proof did he get?"

"Depositions, photographs. It was enough."

"What became of them?"

"I turned them over to Warren when the divorce became final. He destroyed them, I should think."

"You didn't sell them to Little Steve?"

A shocked expression swept over the woman's face. "No! Will you leave or must I call the police?" she said in a voice that trembled with anger.

MacRae lit a cigarette and eyed her thoughtfully.

Her legs were a little sturdy, perhaps, but nice enough looking. Her figure was extraordinarily good for a woman her age—the result of rigid dieting and exercise, he suspected. She had a sleek, well-groomed look, and obviously spent a good deal of time on her appearance.

"Sure," he said, "I'm going, but first, could you tell me where Warren kept his confidential papers?"

"In his study!" she snapped. "He had a wall safe—" She paused and narrowed her eyes at MacRae. "Why? Haven't the police discovered the safe?"

MacRae racked his memory hastily, but he could remember no wall safe in Amiel Warren's study. It must be hidden behind the books.

He said, "Yeh, but it was empty. Did he have a safe deposit box in any name beside his own?"

"I don't know."

"Did you know he was connected with the handbooks?"

She bit her lip. "Really, Mr. MacRae, I don't see how this concerns you. I'm expecting company any minute—"

"One more question," he said. "What kind of person was Corinne?"

Sylvia Warren's jaws clamped together.

"I didn't know her!"

"But surely you'd met her?"

"At my husband's office, yes. She was a small-boned, dark, rather pretty little thing," she admitted grudgingly. "But inclined to plumpness. Curvy. She was very vivacious and helpful, but I got a definite impression of a scheming, busy little mind viciously at work behind—" She caught herself up short. "Perhaps I'm prejudiced," she said stiffly.

MacRae stood up, hat in hand. "Well, thank you for your cooperation, Mrs. Warren," he began when the doorbell rang shrilly.

Mrs. Warren caught her breath and looked as if she'd like to stuff MacRae in the garbage-disposal chute.

MacRae, who was still edgy, wondered if his would-be killers could have followed him again. He didn't think so, because he'd done everything except wade through water to shake any possible tail.

The bell rang again.

Mrs. Warren crossed the room and opened the door. "Why, hello Sam," she said gaily. It was the most amazing about-face MacRae had ever seen. "I was beginning to be afraid you weren't coming."

MacRae saw that it was Sam Jenkins. The layoff man was dressed nattily in slacks, sport coat, and a bow tie. He was smiling at Sylvia Warren. When he caught sight of MacRae, his expression didn't change.

"Sam," said Mrs. Warren, "this is Mr. MacRae. He's just leaving."

"Hello, Jaimie," Jenkins said pleasantly, but his eyes were suddenly wary, and he hunched his shoulders almost imperceptibly—a defensive gesture that was a hangover from his ring days.

"Sam Jenkins!" said MacRae. "I didn't know you and Mrs. Warren were friends."

"Sylvia?" the gambler's smile broadened, but it still didn't reach his eyes. "We've known each other for years."

Sylvia Warren looked bewildered as she stared from face to face. "You—you've met before?"

MacRae laughed and nudged Jenkins in the ribs, learning to his relief that he wasn't carrying a gun. "Hell, we were kids together."

"Just one big happy family," said Mrs. Warren sarcastically.

MacRae said, "Well, glad to've seen you Sammy. I'd better be moving along!"

"No," said Jenkins. "Sit down. I've been trying to get in touch with you all day." He turned to Mrs. Warren. "What about a drink, Sylvia?"

"I've some Tom Collins mix in the refrigerator," she said grudgingly.

"Good." He sat down on the couch, offered MacRae a cigarette, and lit it for him with a flat platinum lighter. He was looking rather pointedly and with obvious amusement at MacRae's discolored and swollen jaw.

"At least you didn't get off without a mark. What did you do out at Monroe Springs? Run amuck?"

"Where'd you hear about it?"

"Don't you know who you tangled with?"

"No," said MacRae shortly.

"Kirt Crump. Cincinnati. He's one of the big boys. He's from the Syndicate. He's down here to find out what's going on."

The laughter went away from MacRae's face, leaving his expression placid, his eyes hooded and watchful.

"What happened after I left?"

"They took Crump to the hospital with a fractured knee. His leg's in a cast and the sawbones say he'll walk with a stiff knee the rest of his life. Bauer—that's the clerk, the fellow you cracked over the head—has a fractured skull."

"So that long drink of water is big time," MacRae said. "I figured he was. Some of his boys tried to cut me down this afternoon."

Jenkins looked suddenly concerned. "You didn't make yourself any too popular nosing around out at the Springs."

"That wire," said MacRae. "It's from the telephone company, isn't it? Stolen?"

"I never said so."

"What have they got, Sam? A wildcat telephone system serving the bookies?"

Jenkins nodded. "Jackson—that's the fellow you kicked in the ear—he used to work for the telephone company. He's installed most of it. Been stringing it up for years. Telephone company doesn't even know it's there. But you've sure put yourself in a hell of a spot, Jaimie. If the police stumble onto that wildcat system, Steve's crowd will think you tipped them off."

MacRae said uncomfortably, "If they haven't found it so far, why should they now?"

Mrs. Warren returned with two tall, frosty glasses on a tray. Jenkins took one, sipped it, and regarded MacRae over the rim.

"Because they've strung some of that stuff downtown and there's a city ordinance against any overhead wires in the downtown fire district. With this drive on to clean out the handbooks, it's bound to be noticed sooner or later."

MacRae suddenly choked on his Tom Collins.

"Why don't you take a vacation?" Jenkins asked. "I mean it. Go down to Florida. They've got a nice summer season now."

"Because I've got to earn a living. What about this Kirt Crump? Is he down here to contact the fellow who's trying to oust Little Steve and take over the organization. What do you think?"

The layoff man frowned.

"I expect he is," he said finally. "I don't know. I haven't heard anything."

"What happens to Little Steve," MacRae asked, "if the Syndicate gives the green light to this other fellow?"

"He'll be out."

"How's Steve going to take that?"

"It doesn't matter how he takes it, he'll still be out. You can't fight the Syndicate. It's too big."

"What about Steve's organization?"

Jenkins said dryly, "It's a business. It's just like any other business. The employees don't quit when they get a new president. The organization'll take their orders from the new boss."

"Why was Warren killed?"

"I don't know, but I can guess. Warren was a snide lawyer—a double-crossing blackmailing rat. But he was a good fix. He had political contacts. He had an ear to the ground. Maybe he found out who was putting the dynamite under him and Little Steve. Do I have to draw you a diagram?"

MacRae glanced at Sylvia Warren. She was sitting on the couch, knees crossed, smoking a cigarette, and staring out the window at a couple of kids playing with a tricycle. If the gambler's description of her ex-husband touched her in any way, her expression didn't reveal it.

MacRae heaved himself to his feet and tugged his

hat squarely on his head.

"Thanks for the tip, Sammy," he said, "and the drink, Mrs. Warren."

She stared at him coldly.

At the door, MacRae paused. "By the way, Sam, what's the lowdown on Coleman? Is he sincere?"

"Henry C., the safety director?" Sam looked disgusted.

"Oh, he's honest. Anybody as loaded as he is can afford to be."

MacRae pulled the door open reluctantly. "I feel like a damn squirrel on the first day of the season, he said plaintively as he let himself out.

CHAPTER 6

When MacRae finally returned to his hotel that night, the clerk stopped him in the lobby.

"There was a call for you, Mr. MacRae."

"Who was it?"

"He didn't say, but he left his number and wanted you to call him back as soon as you came in."

"O.K." MacRae took the slip of paper and went over to the phone on the wall and dialed. He could hear it ringing at the other end. Then the receiver clicked and a hoarse voice said:

"Hockmiller speaking. Hello! Hello!"

MacRae put the receiver quietly back on the hook. He returned to the desk. "If there are any more calls for me," he told the clerk, "I haven't come in yet. Understand?"

The clerk nodded.

Inside his room, MacRae locked the door carefully,

but he didn't turn on the light. He checked the windows, shoved the chair under the knob, undressed in the dark, and rolled into bed.

By the next morning, the swelling in his jaw had gone down but the sooty-looking bruises remained. He unlocked the top drawer of the dresser, took out a holstered revolver wrapped in an oiled rag. It was a beautiful thing in an ugly way, like a coral snake—a .38 Special on a .41 Colt frame, slick and blue-black with a walnut grip. He flipped out the cylinder, stared into the barrel, and wiped it caressingly. Then, buckling the cut-down hip holster around his waist under his coat, he dropped a dozen cartridges in his coat pocket and let himself out.

It was almost nine o'clock when MacRae ambled into the office. He found Ives at her desk sorting the mail. At sight of him, she sat up straight and let her breath go shakily.

"There you are!" she said in a funny voice.

"Sure," said MacRae, pulling up at her tone. "How's the sunburn this morning?"

Ives ignored the question. She pulled her glasses down on her nose and eyed him with growing bitterness over the rims.

"Where have you been?"

"In my room," he said completely mystified. "I went out to breakfast, but—"

"I phoned your hotel," she interrupted grimly. "They told me you weren't in. They said you hadn't been in all night. The clerk didn't seem to think it was strange. I guess he knows you better than I do. But I—after those men tried to kill you yesterday, I was—I acted pretty upset. Mr. Dunn just sent Walker over to your hotel. I've called the police and General Hospital—"

"Good God!" said MacRae. "But I was—" Then he stopped, remembering the orders he had left with the night clerk and began to grin. "I told the clerk to say I hadn't come in if anyone phoned. I didn't think about you calling."

"I tried to get hold of you," she explained stiffly, "to let you know that Mr. Hockmiller phoned this morning." She swallowed suddenly at the memory.

"Yeh. What did he want?"

"He said," said Ives in a tight voice, "that if you didn't get out to see him goddamn quick, he was going to send a couple of his boys for you. He said he was getting goddamn tired of you giving him the goddamn runaround."

MacRae gave her a startled look.

"That's what he said," she said defensively.

The door to Isaac Dunn's private office opened. The manager thrust his head outside and regarded MacRae with anything but pleasure.

"Well, well," he said, "if it isn't the old tomcat. So you finally dragged yourself back."

Ives giggled for there was about MacRae something faintly reminiscent of a big, battle-scarred complacent tomcat.

MacRae scowled.

"Come in here," the manager said, jerking his head at his office. "I want to talk to you."

MacRae went in and sat down. Through the window he could see the spans of the George Rogers Clark Memorial Bridge, black and spidery against the cloudless blue sky. It was going to be another scorcher.

Dunn thrust out his lower lip.

"What are you stirring up, MacRae? I had a call this morning from the Cincinnati office. They wanted to know what the hell I thought I was running down here—the Senate Crime Investigating Committee? We're being hired to find Corinne Hockmiller, MacRae. The handbooks are no concern of ours."

"All right," said MacRae sourly. "Put Walker on it. I've had a bellyful anyway."

Unimpressed, Dunn continued to regard him with his small, bleak gray eyes.

"The truth of the matter is, that you've been on the case since last Friday and you haven't gotten so much as a smell of Corinne."

"If I hadn't it wouldn't be surprising," said MacRae. "Every cop in the country's been on the lookout for her during the past two weeks." He shook out a cigarette and lit it. "But as it happens, I know where she is—approximately."

Dunn leaned forward, a glitter of surprise showing in his eyes.

"Where?"

"Monroe Springs."

"Alive or dead?"

"The odds are that she's dead. Planted around there someplace. Maybe in the lake."

"Have you got enough for us to get the police to drag the lake?"

"It's going to take something pretty damned convincing to get them to stir up trouble at Monroe Springs."

"And you don't have it?"

"Not yet."

"What have you got?"

"A piece of photograph that Corinne autographed. Maggie—Miss Ives picked it up by the incinerator in back of the hotel. It could've been one that Corinne gave Ward Bruton, the stick man out there. But why would he try to destroy it? And he's jumpy as the devil about something. Anyway, I want to look the place over again."

"What's this business about telephone wire that Miss Ives was telling me about? And you getting shot at?"

MacRae ran a thick forefinger inside his collar and stretched his neck uncomfortably.

"Oh, that," he said. "I went out to talk to Bruton on a tip from Little Steve. While we were out there we stumbled across some stolen telephone wire and equipment."

"Where?"

"In the cellar. Unfortunately, we were discovered and—"

"What were you doing in the cellar?"

"Just following a hunch," said MacRae, who figured the less said, the better.

"Go ahead," Dunn prompted acidly.

MacRae gave him an expurgated and boiled-down version of what had taken place Saturday night and Sunday.

"What do you think's in back of all this?" Dunn asked.

"Somebody's fixing to take over the handbooks," MacRae said with a shrug. "But he isn't making his play until he's got the Syndicate on his side."

"Quite likely," Dunn agreed dryly. "It's even more likely that this character killed Big Steve Hockmiller or hired it done. Warren, too, probably, since they were both in his way. But I don't know who he is, and I don't want to know."

"But maybe Corinne did," MacRae interrupted. "She

was close to both Big Steve and Warren."

"All right," said Dunn, "say that she was a threat to whoever's trying to bring off this coup. Suppose he put her out of the way. Our only interest in the affair is to find Corinne or establish her death. It's up to the police to track down her murderer, not us."

"Well, goddamn it," said MacRae irritably, "what do you think I've been trying to do?"

Isaac Dunn drummed his finger tips on the desk top. "I've warned you," he said finally.

On his way to police headquarters, MacRae stopped at the bank and deposited the hundred and fifty dollars in his checking account which brought the total amount to $3,283.50. With the bonds in his safety deposit box, the two pieces of rental property in the colored district, and the house in the West End which he had divided into four efficiency apartments, MacRae estimated that he was worth roughly forty thousand dollars. That was in the inflated currency of the period, he hastened to caution himself.

Sergeant Emberger, in charge of the homicide squad, was a tall, rawboned man only an inch shorter than MacRae. His dark suit bagged, the seat of his pants was shiny, and his straw hat was stained. He bit off a chew of tobacco and stared at MacRae without any great show of affection.

"From what I've been hearing about you," he said, "it looks like you might be my next case."

"Don't get your hopes up, Harry," MacRae said amiably. "How about a cup of coffee?"

"Do you mean you're offering to buy?"

"Sure," said MacRae. "It'll be on the expense account."

"I'll bet it will at that," said the sergeant. He picked

his hat off the desk, and they went out the back way and across the alley to a cafe on the corner, where they took their cups to a booth.

"Well," said Emberger, "go on and pump me."

"What about the bullets in Warren?"

"There weren't any in him. We found them lodged in the books. Thirty-eight caliber. We sent them to the FBI laboratory in Washington. Some hair, too."

"Red hair?"

"Yeh," the sergeant grunted in surprise. "How did you know?"

MacRae told him about the purchases made at Currie's Department Store and the red-haired woman whom the delivery driver said had received them.

Emberger set down his cup so violently that some of the coffee slopped over the rim.

"What put you onto that?" he demanded, his voice laden with suspicion. "What have you been holding out on us, MacRae?"

"Nothing," said MacRae complacently, refraining from mentioning the Currie's price tag that Ives had found in the wastebasket. "Just a routine piece of work. I'm surprised you overlooked it."

The sergeant snorted.

"Obviously a woman had been staying at Warren's house," MacRae explained. "There were—"

"What was so damned obvious about it?"

"Little things. The scent of toilet water, a few grains of perfumed powder on the dresser. Women always think they need something. I figured if she had stayed there any time she would have bought a few things. What was more natural than for her to call up and have them sent out? It didn't take me long to find out Warren had a charge account at Currie's. So—"

SWITCHEROO 99

"Yeh," said the sergeant bitterly. "You're a real bright boy. When were these deliveries made?"

"Last Wednesday. Two days before he was killed. The driver's name is Nick something-or-other. He said she was a good-looking, red-haired babe."

"Well," said the sergeant, starting to edge out of the booth, "I have to work at my job."

"Wait a minute," said MacRae. "What about fingerprints?"

"Too many of them. Nothing conclusive."

"What did you find in the wall safe?"

Sergeant Emberger sat down again. "What wall safe?" he asked in a gentle voice.

"Behind the books in the study. Do you mean you overlooked it?" MacRae regarded him pityingly.

The sergeant got ominously to his feet. "Where did you learn about the safe, MacRae?"

"From Warren's ex-wife."

"She didn't say anything about it to us when we talked to her."

"Maybe you didn't ask her. Mind if I tag along when you open it?"

"Of course not," Emberger said with exaggerated politeness. "What would we do without you? Perhaps you also know the combination?"

"No," said MacRae amiably, "Warren was the only one who was supposed to know that."

With the sirens clearing traffic ahead of them, it took them only a few minutes to drive out to Warren's place. They found the safe without trouble behind a section of false books, but the combination wasn't necessary.

It was a barrel-type safe, set in the wall, and the door was slightly ajar and the safe was empty.

Sergeant Emberger swore long and profanely while the fingerprint man fussed around with his powder.

MacRae shook his head gloomily. "Any prints?"

"Yeh. Couple pretty clear ones," the fingerprint man said.

"The way my luck's running," said the sergeant bitterly, "they're probably Warren's."

When at length they got back to City Hall, a police car was pulling out of the alley in the rear. It swung south on Sixth Street, tires complaining, and shot down to Jefferson, where a low moan of its siren cleared traffic at the intersection.

MacRae had recognized the sour, lumpy features of Major Bridwell, chief of detectives, in the back seat. There had been a uniformed police captain with him and two plainclothes detectives besides the driver.

As Sergeant Emberger turned into the alley from which the prowl car had just shot, MacRae saw Colonel Hendricks standing with Safety Director Coleman at the head of the steps. They were watching the receding police car. Then they turned and went into the back door of City Hall.

"Hey," said MacRae, "something up?"

Sergeant Emberger shrugged, but his eyes were glittering with curiosity. As they rolled to a stop, the sergeant jumped out and ran inside.

MacRae followed him into the detectives' room. The assistant chief of detectives, Major Bridwell's secretary, and a couple of plainclothesmen were talking in low voices.

They stopped when they caught sight of MacRae.

"What's going on?" he asked.

The loudspeaker on the wall broke into raucous speech. "Car 68 go to Shelby and Jefferson. Car 68 go to Shelby and Jefferson."

Major Bridwell's secretary rubbed his nose and regarded MacRae sourly.

"It's a raid," he said.

"Knocking over another bookie?"

"Yeh."

"It must be a big one."

"It is," the secretary said.

MacRae was not entirely satisfied, but he saw that he was going to get no more information out of them. He went across the hall to the Identification Bureau, where he found Sergeant Franck.

Franck said there wasn't anything new on Corinne Hockmiller. He said so far as he knew, the excitement was just another raid. Though he understood the bookie was an important one. Perhaps that accounted for the big brass' interest.

Swearing under his breath, MacRae descended the steps to the street. As he reached the pavement, he heard the wail of a siren. Then he saw the patrol wagon barreling east on Jefferson with cars pulling to the curb ahead of it. To the south, away from the river, another siren lifted its voice faintly, sounding like a dog howling in the distance.

MacRae listened to the troubled wailing, unable to put down an uncomfortable sense of alarm that welled up inside of him. At length, he shrugged irritably and crossed the street and cut through the courthouse lawn toward Fifth. The sirens were fading into silence. The flow of cars and pedestrians had already resumed their interrupted aimless scurry. Heat waves shimmered up from the concrete gray sidewalks.

MacRae found the name on the fly-specked directory

in the lobby.

Youngblood Detective Agency........418

A Negro girl in a soiled smock took him up in a decrepit elevator to the fourth floor of the rundown office building. The hall was quiet, the floor gritty underfoot. Four-eighteen was around the corner from the elevator. "Youngblood Detective Agency" was lettered in black on the dirty frosted pane.

MacRae opened the door and went inside a tiny waiting room not much bigger than a closet. A lamp glowed on a battered end table. Two squashed and worn upholstered chairs practically filled the room, which was otherwise empty except for an unpleasant smell of dust and stale tobacco smoke.

He could hear a buzzer. Then it stopped. Something thumped on the floor and the door to the inner office opened. "Hello, Jake," MacRae said.

The man in the doorway quit smiling at sight of his visitor. He was a sharp-faced, long nosed little man, not much bigger than a jockey.

"Aren't you going to ask me in?" MacRae said genially.

"What do you want?"

Anxiety was apparent in his thin voice—anxiety and a corroding hate. By the grace of an uncle who was a city alderman, Jake Youngblood had been on the police force at the same time as MacRae. Jake had been dismissed for accepting bribes. His grafting had been so transparent that not even the uncle had been able to save him, though his influence had kept him out of the penitentiary. It had been MacRae who had collected most of the evidence against him.

"A little information," said MacRae, pushing inside.

The inner office wasn't much bigger than the waiting

room. A battered oak desk backed against the window and beside it squatted a huge, old-fashioned safe. A couple of scarred green metal filing cabinets were shoved against the sickly green walls. MacRae sat down in front of the desk, while Youngblood seated himself behind it.

Without any preliminaries, MacRae said, "Mrs. Warren hired you to get evidence against her husband."

"What of it?" said the little man, curling his lip, but he couldn't erase the anxiety from his eyes.

"We seem to be getting nowhere fast," MacRae said mildly. "I'm buying, Jake. I'm willing to pay fifty dollars for the right kind of information."

"You can take your money," Jake snapped bitterly, "and shove—"

"Not interested in fifty dollars," MacRae cut him off, his voice hardening. "The blackmail racket must be pretty good." He leaned across the desk suddenly and his arm shot out and he grabbed the private detective by the shirt front.

"Jake," he said, "you're making it mighty hard for me to do business with you. Maybe I'd do better to use the kind of language you understand."

Jake sputtered helplessly, his eyes shiny with panic. MacRae gave him a gentle shake that made his teeth rattle. "What did you get on Warren?"

"I didn't get nothing on him."

"You're a liar," said MacRae. "He was playing around with Corinne Hockmiller, Big Steve's wife."

"No! Corinne was hot for a fellow by the name of Ward Bruton. There wasn't anything like that between her and Warren."

MacRae turned loose of him. "No," he said. "Then on what grounds did Sylvia Warren get her divorce?"

"I don't know," Jake said doggedly. "Ask her."

"I did. She said that you secured evidence for her—"

"I tell you there wasn't any!" Jake interrupted. "It was strictly business between Warren and Corinne."

MacRae's battered face grew suddenly placid. "Business," he said softly, and there was no depth to his eyes, no expression in them. "What was this business?"

Jake looked as if he could have bitten out his tongue. "He was a lawyer," he said uncomfortably. "He looked after her interests, that was all."

"You'll have to do better than that," said MacRae.

Jake's Adam's apple bobbed up and down in his skinny neck as he swallowed.

"All right," he said in a half-strangled voice. "But don't tell anybody where you got this." He opened the top drawer of his desk. "Take a look for yourself."

The dull gleam of blued metal caught MacRae's suspicious eyes a moment too soon. He lunged up from his chair and came half across the desk as if someone had stabbed him with a needle. His fist smashed Jake on the jaw.

The little detective went over backwards, chair and all. The automatic flew up in the air. The back of Jake's skull hit the window sill with an ugly crack.

MacRae went right over the desk after him, but Jake was out cold. He scooped up the automatic—a .32 Colt—and dropped it into his pocket. Then he turned to the desk and began to go through the drawers.

Then he went to the safe but it was locked, which was disappointing. So were the filing cabinets, but they opened with a key. He searched Jake, turning the contents of his pockets onto the desk: a billfold containing two hundred and forty-two dollars, a Parker fountain pen, an envelope with a negative in it, which he pocketed after examining it against the light. He couldn't be sure, but it looked as if it had been taken on the river and showed what seemed to be a couple of figures sprawled on the deck of a boat.

He found the keys finally in a flat leather key case and after making sure that Jake wasn't likely to disturb him for a while, unlocked the cabinets. The files held the records of cases carefully labeled and put away in folders. Divorce cases, for the most part, some skip tracing, petty thievery by employees. But there was no folder labeled Warren or Hockmiller or Bruton.

He eyed the massive, impregnable safe sourly.

"Well, Jaimie," he said, "safe cracking's not one of your talents."

Making sure that he had the envelope with the negative in it, he let himself out, locked the doors behind him, dropped the key case in his pocket, and walked down the four floors to the street.

He reached the sidewalk about the same time as the late edition of the evening paper. He bought one from the man on the corner, glanced at the headlines and felt his stomach turn over uncomfortably.

The headlines said:

BOOKIE PHONE NETWORK
CUT OUT OF BUSINESS

and under that in only slightly smaller type:

8 Miles of 'Wildcat' Lines
Chopped Down By Police;
Handbooks Blacked Out

There were a couple of pictures, one of a uniformed policeman on a ladder, cutting a telephone wire.

MacRae leaned weakly against the plate-glass window of a jewelry store and read the article, a hollow feeling growing where his stomach ought to be.

All over the downtown area today, handbooks were blacked out as vice squad officers, accompanied by telephone linesmen, cut down an illegal communication setup containing at least eight miles of wire. It was the stiffest jolt dealt the handbooks since Safety Director, Henry C. Coleman, last November ordered the telephone company to yank all lines serving the bookies.

Nine main circuits were severed, and many more cuts made as police, aided by telephone linesmen, traced the wires back and forth down the three-block stretch on Jefferson between Third and Brook. Police said it was uncertain where the lines originated.

The State manager for Southern Bell Telephone & Telegraph Company described the operations as "a great headache for us." The hijacking, he explained, worked something like this:

"Certain unscrupulous people who can't obtain telephone service for their rackets, contact legitimate phone subscribers and offer money for use of their phones. Then workmen, sometimes ex-telephone company employees, string and hook up the lines so bookmakers can have numerous lines running from their switchboards."

Then in bold type:

TIP-OFF REVEALS EXTENT
OF WILDCAT NETWORK

An anonymous telephone call led police to arrest Pete Jackson, 44-year-old electrician and former employee of the telephone company. Jackson was caught actually installing an illegal telephone line. He was charged with knowingly receiving stolen property when the wire he was using was identified as property of the telephone company. His trial is set for Saturday in police court.

There was more on the back page, including a cut of Pete Jackson, the lineman whom the police had arrested. MacRae recognized him instantly, as the fellow whom he had kicked in the ear out at Monroe Springs last Saturday.

A car backfired on the street in front of him. MacRae jumped as if he'd been shot. There was no use getting rattled, he told himself. What he needed was a drink to settle his nerves. He folded the paper, shoved it in his pocket, and started in search of a bar.

On his way back to the office, MacRae stopped in at the Starre Studios. With the aid of a ten-dollar bill and not too much trouble he learned what he already knew: namely, that Corinne Hockmiller had had her picture taken, that the negatives were on file in case of a reorder, that he could secure a print for a small additional fee.

MacRae parted reluctantly with another ten, and after a while he was handed three five-by-seven studio portraits still warm from the drier. He was also given a print from the negative which he had lifted from Jake Youngblood.

The photographs of Corinne had been taken almost a year before, while her husband was still alive. She looked very much as he had expected: an exceedingly pretty, plump little brunette with very fair skin; a little older than she appeared in the police circular; a little wiser and harder perhaps. Her dark eyes looked larger and appeared vaguely dissatisfied. Two of the photographs were full face, one smiling, the other with features in repose. The third was a semi-profile. MacRae had the feeling that he was looking at a dead woman.

But it was the picture that he had found on Youngblood that gave him the greatest shock. The photograph showed two girls taking a sun bath on the deck of a cabin cruiser. One of the girls he recognized instantly as Corinne Hockmiller, though he could scarcely believe it. The angle at which the picture had been taken made her look thinner than in her studio portraits.

It was the second girl, though, that really startled him. Emily Franklin! Emily Franklin, the girl who occupied the apartment next to Corinne at the Tower Arms. The girl who had said that she knew Corinne only to speak to.

"Nodding acquaintance!" he muttered explosively and the photographer—a Bohemian-looking man in a beret—edged off uneasily.

Part of one side of the boat was visible as far down as a porthole. He could barely make out a name painted on the side in black letters. *The Mermaid*, it said.

The job of finding out who owned the boat shouldn't be too difficult. A cruiser that size would be well-known on the river. Meanwhile, he intended to have a word with Emily Franklin.

CHAPTER 7

Emily Franklin met him at the door of Arstark's Grill with an eager, warm, and friendly smile. The effect was signally gratifying as she seemed sincerely delighted to see MacRae.

"May I—" she began, then she recognized him and her face fell. "You! What do you want?"

"A little talk."

"But I'm working."

MacRae let his eyes run around the grill. The rose-colored lights were so dim that it was like trying to see through a fog. There was a bar at the right and padded booths in back, surrounded by low partitions. A broad, curving staircase led up to the private dining rooms above.

"You're off in a few minutes. Six, you said."

"Yes," she admitted, biting her lip. "But—"

"I'll wait," he said, "right here. And I want the truth this time." And pulling the picture out of his pocket, he let her see it clearly.

She stared at it in perplexity. Then a look of complete consternation swept across her face.

"But that's impossible!"

"Sure," said MacRae. "After all, you only knew Corinne to speak to." He put the photograph back in his pocket.

Emily Franklin regarded him out of dazed yellowish-brown eyes. With a chuckle, MacRae went over to the bar and started to order a bourbon and soda until he saw the price.

"Holy mackerel!" he said. "Give me a small beer."

Emily Franklin's relief came on promptly at six, and Emily disappeared, only to return in a few moments with her handbag. She was wearing a white blouse with eggshell colored lace around the low, square neckline; a beige skirt, high-heeled open work shoes; nylon stockings with dark heels.

She gave MacRae a faintly appalled sidelong glance as they went through the door.

"This way." He steered her toward the river. "I'm parked on the wharf."

They walked in silence the four blocks to the waterfront. The river looked as placid as a lake, orange peels, a few planks and a cabbage leaf floating at the water's edge. The Colgate clock across the river in Clarksville, said 6:47.

MacRae helped the girl into his car and got in the other side.

"Where to?"

She seemed to have made a decision, for she glanced at him with a quizzical smile.

"Let's go up to my apartment. We can—ah—talk better there. Wouldn't you like to?"

"You bet," said MacRae enthusiastically.

The third-floor apartment had been closed all day and was as hot and stifling as a brick kiln. MacRae shucked off his coat and hat. He lowered himself with a grunt onto the sofa and mopped his face with his handkerchief.

Emily went around opening windows. In a minute, she returned and planted herself in front of him, hands on hips.

"You want information and I want that picture. There's no reason why we can't get together."

"Fine," said MacRae.

SWITCHEROO III

"Then just as soon as I slip into something comfortable," she said, "I'll tell you whatever you want to know."

MacRae wiped the sweat off his face and settled back with an expectant grin. "Something comfortable!" How many times had he read that phrase. Whenever the girl said to the detective, "Let me slip into something comfortable," everybody knew exactly what to expect.

Highly amused, he lit a cigarette and puffed away with satisfaction. He heard the bedroom door open, and he swung around with a gleam in his eyes. Then the gleam flickered and went out.

Emily was wearing a man's white broadcloth shirt, with the tails hanging out, blue jeans and red sandals. Her hair was pinned up on top of her head and her face had a brown, freshly-scrubbed look. The only concession she had made to MacRae's presence had been lipstick; and that, he suspected, had been the result of no more than force of habit.

"You don't know how good it feels," she said, oblivious to his punctured complacency, "to get into something sloppy and just relax."

MacRae stared at her in stony silence. At length, he cleared his throat. "Now then," he said, in a rather cool voice, "about that snapshot—"

She seated herself on the sofa beside him, so that she was facing him, and laid a hand on his knee.

"Honest, I haven't known Corinne long. Only since she moved here. That was about six months ago. Right after her husband was killed. You believe that, don't you?"

"Sure," he said.

She looked searchingly into his eyes. "I'm being

honest. I thought at first that if I—I made a play for you—" she dropped her lashes. "You know what I mean. Some men are—well— But I don't think that would work so good with you."

"Hell fire!" said MacRae. "You give up too quick!"

She laughed and shook her head. "No, I might as well tell you the truth. I get a lot of calls to go on parties. I don't mean that I'm a call girl. It's not that—that—"

MacRae raised his eyebrows unpleasantly.

"They're real parties," she was quick to assure him, "and the men are pretty influential people. Real big shots. You'd be surprised if you knew—"

She caught herself up short.

"Anyway, they get pretty raw sometimes. If there ever was any trouble, well, that would finish me." She shivered. "I mean, I might actually end up in the river if—if it was serious enough. You can see why I got so upset when I saw that picture. If it got in the hands of the wrong people and they used it for blackmail—" She shivered again. "You think I'm kidding, don't you?"

"No," said MacRae, whose expression had grown placidly watchful.

"You couldn't tell me who you got it from?"

"Not yet."

She caught her lower lip between small white teeth.

"Well," she said, "when Corinne moved in next door, we naturally got to know each other pretty well. She didn't have much money, and I told her about the parties. She wanted me to take her along."

"Did Corinne go on these parties often?" he asked.

"All the time. But I don't think she had much fun. She'd be quiet as a mouse one time, then the next she'd talk your head off. It was funny about the way

SWITCHEROO

she lost weight too. All the while she was here, it just seemed to melt off. She wasn't anything but skin and bones when she disappeared."

"Sick?"

"I don't know. She always said she felt all right. But she acted like she was scared to death half the time."

"Anybody come to see her?"

"Oh, yes. Her lawyer. You know, that fellow who was killed the other day."

"How friendly was she with him?"

"Friendly!" Emily gave a brittle laugh. "She hated his guts. Whenever that shyster showed up, she was upset for days afterward."

"Why?"

Emily shook her head.

"What about Ward Bruton?"

"Oh, that was different. She ran around with him a lot. But I never got the idea that she was passionately fond of the guy."

"Sort of a cold proposition, eh?" said MacRae. "What about the picture?"

Her yellow-brown eyes darkened. "That—that must have been taken while we were on an overnight party just before Corinne disappeared. It was a big cabin cruiser, you know, and we went up the Ohio to Cincinnati and back."

"Who does the cruiser belong to?"

Emily flashed him a frightened glance and shook her head.

"Don't be a fool!" he said brutally. "The name of the cruiser was *The Mermaid*. It'll take me about fifteen minutes to find out who the owner is. Do you want me to go to him?"

Emily clutched his arm in genuine fright.

"No! Don't do that! I'll tell you!" She had come halfway up on her knees on the couch.

Being farsighted, MacRae kept drawing his head back uncomfortably.

"Please!" she begged shakily. "Promise me you'll give me the picture and won't let anyone else see it."

She began to tremble. Her lips were parted slightly in fright, showing her small, even white teeth. Then she pulled herself against him convulsively, saying, "Please, please," with her mouth against his face.

"Goddamn it!" MacRae sputtered, her hair getting in his mouth. "Who does the launch belong to?"

She let out her breath in a long, unsteady sob. "Henry Coleman."

"The Safety Director!" MacRae almost shouted.

"Y-yes."

"Go on," he said grimly, "I want to hear the rest of this." He started to push her away so that he could get to his feet. He wanted to see her expression as she talked, but she clung to him frantically and wouldn't look at him. "O.K., O.K.," he said. "Tell me about this party."

"We—we went up the river to Cincinnati," she said.

"Who?"

"Hen and I. That's what I call Henry Coleman," she said and giggled nervously. "And—and Corinne and Mort Stevenson. Just the four of us. It was Mort who took the picture, I suppose, while Corinne and I were sunning ourselves on top the cabin. He's a camera crank and—"

"Who's Mort Stevenson?"

"I—I don't know him very well. He says he's a retired broker."

"What happened at Cincinnati?" he asked.

"Nothing. Hen called up some people and they came down to the boat. Everybody got plastered. I mean really plastered. The girl from Cincinnati fell overboard. And when we fished her out, we were afraid she'd drowned. Everybody took turns giving her artificial respiration. At least, the men did."

She began to giggle hysterically.

"What's so funny about that?" said MacRae who had a mental picture of a bunch of drunks making a lark out of giving artificial respiration to a half-drowned girl.

"They had the wrong girl," she was unable to stop giggling. "The g-g-girl who'd fallen in had gone to a cabin to get off her wet clothes. They were giving Corinne artificial respiration. She'd passed out."

She slid weakly onto MacRae's lap where she lay staring up into his face.

"That's all. Honest. But if it should get out. The safety director! Please, where did you get that picture?"

"Jake Youngblood, a cheap, chiseling private detective."

She flinched, the blood draining from her face. "The negative," she whispered. "What about the negative?"

"I've got it. Not with me. In a safe place."

She relaxed limply, gave a long, shuddering sigh of relief. Her eyes were yellow. Her full lips parted slightly. Her quick shallow breathing made her breasts tremble.

"Will you," she asked unsteadily, "will you give me the negative?"

"You're too anxious to get your hands on it," he said in a flat voice. "What are you holding back?"

She lay still, the invitation in her eyes slowly being crowded out by doubt and perplexity. When she spoke, it was almost with a note of panic.

"There wasn't anything else. Really."

"Who were the people from Cincinnati who came down to the boat?"

"I don't know. I didn't pay much attention to their names. I—I was pretty tight. Honest!"

MacRae's expression was suddenly savage. He shoved the girl off his lap and got to his feet.

"Coleman will remember," he said and reached for his coat.

Emily scrambled off the couch and caught his arm. "No!" she begged wildly. "I'll tell you. There was a girl called Angie. She was the one who fell in the river—and an awfully tall man. His name was Crump—"

"Kirt Crump!" he exclaimed in spite of himself.

"Yes. Do you know him?"

MacRae's eyes were like flat blue disks. "We've met," he said, adding nothing. "Who else?"

"There was another man," she said. "But I didn't hear his name and nobody paid any attention to him. I—I think he was sort of a bodyguard to Mr. Crump."

"What did Crump and Coleman talk about?"

"Why—why nothing in particular. It was just a party."

MacRae continued to stare at her.

"Honest!" she said, her eyes begging him to believe her. "They didn't say anything that I heard. I'm leveling with you."

He said, "What happened to Corinne after she passed out?"

Emily began to tremble, first her knees, then her hands.

The skin of her face looked tight and yellowish like an old drumhead.

"N-nothing."

MacRae took a step toward her and his hands closed brutally on her shoulders. "Don't lie to me!"

Emily cried out in pain. She managed to squirm out of the shirt, the buttons popping, and jerked away frantically. She ran behind the sofa. MacRae dropped the shirt and moved toward her without haste. She backed into the corner, oblivious to the fact that she was naked to the waist. Her breasts rose spasmodically at each breath as her lungs strained for air. She put out a hand as if to stop MacRae's inexorable advance. Suddenly her face seemed to crumble and she went to pieces.

"I don't know! I don't know!" she gasped.

"What do you mean, you don't know?"

"I never saw her again."

She sank down on the sofa, clutching MacRae's coat. "Everything's terribly hazy. They told me the next morning that she got sore and walked out on the party." Her words, shaky and almost incoherent, rushed over themselves in her urgency to persuade him.

"Walked out?"

"Yes. They said she had friends in Cincinnati. I haven't seen her since."

"She never came back here?"

She shook her head dumbly.

"Did you actually see her leave the boat?"

"No, no."

"Did you see her after she came to?"

"I can't remember."

"Think!" he roared savagely.

"Oh, God," she wailed, "I can't remember. I can't!"

"Then the last time you remember seeing her," he

hammered implacably, "she'd passed out and the men were giving her artificial respiration?"

"I don't know. Yes—yes, I guess so."

"In the cabin or on deck?"

"I can't remember." She began to cry, not making any noise except for the sobbing intake of her breath.

He kept at her, but it was hopeless. She repeated over and over again, "I can't remember. I can't remember."

He straightened his coat, set his hat squarely on his head and stared at the girl morosely. She was lying face down on the couch, her face buried in the cushion, her naked shoulders shaking from the uncontrolled violence of her sobbing. The corners of his mouth twitched downward with distaste as he quietly let himself out.

CHAPTER 8

It was still early, scarcely nine o'clock, when MacRae finally got back to his hotel. The lobby looked oddly disreputable, as if he were seeing it through someone else's eyes: the worn red carpet with the warp showing through in spots, the shiny squashed leather chairs, the battered desk where the clerk, behind his grill, was bending over the evening paper.

He asked the clerk if there had been any calls for him. There hadn't been, and he lumbered on down the hall.

The dim light in the corridor cut a swath out of the blackness of his room as he opened the door. He went inside, closing the door behind him, and groped for the light switch.

SWITCHEROO

It came on with a click.

A sharp voice said, "Hold it!"

MacRae jerked as if he had been kicked in the stomach.

There was a man sitting on the edge of his bed, grinning. He was a big, young man with thick lips and milky blue eyes. His grayish-green suit fit too tightly and his hat was pushed back. His feet, in brown pointed oxfords, were planted solidly on the floor.

He was holding a .45 Colt automatic in his fist. MacRae could see his knuckles, raw and swollen looking, as he held the gun tight.

MacRae sucked in his stomach and his flesh tried to crawl away from the line of that round black hole.

"That's him," a lighter voice said.

MacRae turned his head cautiously and saw the second man—a slight, stoop-shouldered fellow with his hat brim shading his eyes. He was sitting in the chair by the window. He, too, had a gun. He waved it carelessly and said, "Put your hands on top of your head."

Reluctantly, MacRae raised his hands, locking his fingers above his hat, mashing the crown.

"Frisk him, Pinky," said the sharp-faced man by the window.

Pinky rose from the bed and approached MacRae warily. He was still grinning and MacRae could see the scar tissue covering his cheekbones. One of his pale red eyebrows was split by a white scar and his nose was thick and flattened.

He ran his hands expertly over MacRae and tossed the .38 to the coverlet.

"He's clean," he said, backing off.

The sharp-faced man got to his feet and jerked his

head at the window. "You come with us," he said. "Don't give us no trouble." The blind was drawn and he pulled it up and slipped through the window like a shadow.

MacRae's lips were stiff as he moved over to the window, which opened onto the alley. Pinky stayed about six feet behind him, his milky-blue eyes watchful. MacRae lifted the blind and saw they had forced the window to enter. He got his legs across the sill and dropped heavily to the ground.

"Move along!" said the sharp-faced man from the shadows.

MacRae heard Pinky's feet hit the brick-paved alley. They closed in on either side of him and gave him a shove in the direction of the street.

Against the pale glow of the alley's mouth, MacRae could see a car silhouetted. The red eye of a cigarette suddenly arched from the car's window and hit the bricks with a spatter of sparks.

"Get in front," said the hatchet-faced man.

MacRae obediently climbed in beside the waiting driver. Then the car moved out of the alley and turned onto the asphalt.

"Give you any trouble?" said the driver.

"I could a took him by myself," said Pinky from the back seat.

MacRae didn't say anything.

The room was in the sub-basement of the Venice—a small, bare room without any windows and only one door. MacRae was sitting on a battered horsehair sofa against the gray concrete wall. His eyes were swollen and his chin drooped against his chest. His white shirt front was spattered with blood. His face was bruised and swollen and bloody. The man called Pinky was holding him upright with a fist twisted in his collar.

Little Steve Hockmiller was straddling a chair, staring at MacRae with somber, hooded eyes. His gaunt bony face made him look more than ever like some farmer.

"He ain't out!" said Pinky. He slapped MacRae's face with his open palm, grabbed him by the hair, and jerked up his head.

From between the swollen slits of his eyes, MacRae stared back at them with a raw, dazed hatred.

Steve said, "Can you hear me, MacRae?"

MacRae mumbled something that might have been "yes."

"Who put you up to it?" Steve said in a monotonous voice.

"You sold me out, MacRae. Don't be a fool. Who is it?"

MacRae didn't say anything.

Pinky drew back his fist and drove it into MacRae's face. MacRae fell back, his head cracking against the wall. Then he toppled over sideways onto the couch.

The sharp-faced man said, "Ah," leaning forward.

Hockmiller swore. "Goddamn it, Pinky," he said, "you'll kill him."

"Not this guy," said Pinky. "He can take it. He's tough." He grabbed MacRae by the shirt front, wrenched him upright, and began to slap his face. The blows cracked like pistol shots.

MacRae's eyes opened again.

"Hold it," said Steve. He got up and stood in front of MacRae.

"Who's the bastard that's trying to muscle in? Who is it?" MacRae's eyes refused to focus.

In a sudden paroxysm of rage, Hockmiller hit him

in the face. MacRae fell over again and rolled off the couch onto the concrete floor. Hockmiller began to kick him in the side.

MacRae was barely able to get his eyes open. The light dazzled him. The room swam into a fuzzy sort of focus. It was like a room full of water. Somebody was holding him up.

The man who held him had a grinning ugly face and milk-blue eyes. He kept slapping MacRae's face.

MacRae tried to push him away.

Voices were saying: "Why did you double-cross me? Who did you sell out to?" They said it over and over again. The voices reached him through a sea of pain and then drifted farther away. Steve Hockmiller's face suddenly seemed to expand before his eyes like a face painted on a balloon. "Get the pliers!"

The voices retreated again and the room grew slowly clearer. He could make out Hockmiller and the sharp-faced man standing by the door. He felt numb and the light hurt his eyes.

What was he doing here? What was happening? He tried to move his arm and groaned. But the sharp pain stimulated his memory.

They thought he knew who was trying to give Little Steve the boot. They thought that he was working for the fellow that was trying to take over the handbooks . . .

The door opened and Pinky appeared in the entrance. The men all turned and looked at him. Then MacRae could see them grow bigger and bigger as they approached, and then they were towering above him.

Pinky grabbed his arm. MacRae tried to kick him,

SWITCHEROO

but his foot scarcely left the floor. Something fastened on one of his fingers.

"Damn!" said Pinky, drawing back in disgust, "The guy's out again."

When MacRae returned to consciousness once more, the room was empty. He was lying on the horsehair sofa with the light burning down into his unprotected eyes.

He didn't know how long he'd been in the room. He didn't know whether it was night or day. After two unsuccessful efforts, he got to his feet. Halfway to the door, he collapsed again.

He crawled the rest of the way, pulled himself upright by the knob. The door was locked.

Sobbing weakly, he slid down in a heap. At length, he raised his head shakily and his eyes fastened on one of the chairs. He began to crawl toward the chair.

It took him a long time and he had to gather his strength, but he finally managed to worry off one of the legs. Painfully, he got to his feet and struck at the glittering electric bulb on its naked wire. At the fourth attempt, he hit it. The light went out with a pop. Slivers of glass tinkled on the concrete floor in the darkness.

MacRae chuckled crazily. He started for the door, fell down, and crawled the rest of the way. When he found the door, he crouched beside it like a sick, wounded animal . . . waiting.

He had dozed off when the sound of a key in the lock roused him. He forced himself to his feet, and panic gripped him. Raising the club overhead, he waited in the darkness. He was afraid that he didn't have enough strength to wield the club.

The door swung inward. Framed in the entrance, with the light behind him, was the sharp-faced man. He had a cup of coffee in one hand and a half-eaten sandwich in the other.

At sight of the darkened interior, he came to a dead stop. "What the hell!" he muttered around a mouthful of food.

MacRae hit him. He brought the chair leg down with the strength of desperation. The coffee cup shattered on the floor, splashing hot coffee into MacRae's shoes. The sharp faced man began to sag, to buckle at the knees.

MacRae hit him again and again until a gleam of sanity penetrated the fog of hate and fear. He got hold of the limp figure by an arm and dragged it back into the darkness. He came out, threw the chair leg into the room and closed the door.

He was in a large pillared room with a ramp which led down to double overhead doors and the river. On the other side of the ramp was another door. MacRae tried to run, but only managed a staggering walk. He felt as if he was in a slow-motion dream. The harder he strained, the further away the door seemed to get.

When he reached it, he found it was locked. He leaned against the door, sobbing in frustration. Then he saw that it was secured by a bolt. With trembling fingers that felt like sausages, he worked at the bolt. Somehow, he got it open, pulled back the door, and staggered out into the night air.

It was late, almost daylight, the stars glittering faintly against the paling sky. A long flight of concrete steps led up the river bank to the parking lot beside the night club. He began to climb them, crawling on his hands and knees.

There were only two cars left in the parking lot and they were beaded with dew. He lurched past them and went on across the lot to the highway. He began to walk down the middle of the blacktop road, not knowing whether he was headed toward Louisville or not.

After a while he saw headlights bearing down on him. He stumbled out in front of the car and tried to wave his arms. The last sound in his ears was the squealing of tires on the asphalt.

MacRae regarded the room blearily. The walls were a pale gray-green. Three gaudy bouquets sat in vases on a chest. The window was open, curtains asway in a pleasant breeze that fanned his bruised, swollen face. A nurse's aide in a black-and-white striped uniform was fussing with the flowers.

He tried to move, groaned out loud, and abandoned the idea.

The nurse's aide, an apple-cheeked homely girl looked around quickly. "You're awake," she said. "I'll get the nurse."

In a moment a thin, rather haggard young woman marched through the door. Sticking a thermometer in his mouth, she picked up his wrist.

"How long have I been here?" MacRae mumbled around the thermometer.

"You're not supposed to talk." In her crisp white uniform she was very business-like. MacRae took the thermometer out of his mouth.

"How long have I been here?"

She frowned and put the thermometer back. "Two days. No more questions now."

"Two days!" MacRae said thickly. "Listen, I've got to

talk to Isaac Dunn at Gibbs & Stockpole."

"He'll be here this afternoon," the nurse said.

MacRae subsided. He didn't feel up to arguing anyway. The nurse took the thermometer out of his mouth, glanced at it, and shook it down. She was about to leave when the door opened again and Sergeant Emberger stuck his head inside.

"Well, well," he said, "if it ain't the bull of the Pampas. They told me at the desk that you'd come out of it. How're you feeling?"

MacRae grunted.

The nurse said indignantly, "The doctor left strict orders that the patient was not to be disturbed—"

"Just two questions," the sergeant said defensively. "I've been sitting on my tail out there on and off for two days now."

MacRae said feebly, "What the hell do you want? You're homicide. I'm not dead yet."

"I'm going to call the Mother Superior," the nurse began angrily.

Sergeant Emberger grinned. "Who worked you over? Some guy in a truck said you staggered in front of him out by the Venice. We thought it was a hit-and-run case until we got a good look at you."

"Couple of Steve's boys."

The sergeant took a police photo of the sharp-faced man out of his pocket and showed it to MacRae. "This one of 'em?"

MacRae tried to nod but regretted it instantly. "Yeh," he said. "Who is he?"

"Bernie Benadotte. What did you do to him?"

"Nothing. Why?"

The sergeant looked disappointed. "We fished him out of the river above Towhead Island. He'd hung up on a snag. Somebody had caved in his skull with a club. That somebody wouldn't have been you, would it?"

"Then he's dead?"

The sergeant snorted.

MacRae said "Ah," in a satisfied tone and closed his eyes. "Did you kill him or didn't you?" said the sergeant.

But MacRae gave no sign that he heard him. His bruised, lumpy, and unshaven face was strangely benign. Then he began to snore gently.

Sergeant Emberger got to his feet, his hat in his hand. He stared down at MacRae for a long moment, his brow furrowed in suspicion. At length, he tiptoed out and closed the door softly behind himself.

Isaac Dunn said in his precise voice: "Forget it. There's no use to give it to the Cincinnati office. Steve Hockmiller has taken a powder. We don't have a client."

MacRae stared at the manager somberly. Dunn was sitting in the chair beside the bed with his hat on his knees and his bald crown gleaming in the light from the bedside lamp. His fat little face was as still and unresponsive as a mask. The smoke from his cigar writhed upward in a slow motion, drowning the hospital smell of iodoform.

"How come?" MacRae asked finally. "Why did Steve pull out?"

"The Venice was raided. It's closed up tight as a drum."

"On account of me?"

Dunn's lips twitched in a meager smile.

"You gave them a good excuse. They've been waiting

for a chance to knock him over. He's finished in this town. His organization is shot to hell." He puffed thoughtfully at the cigar. "Big Steve was the brains. Little Steve never was and never will be anything but a hooligan. I wouldn't be surprised if he didn't turn mean after this."

MacRae spoke with difficulty. "He hasn't cleared out. He's lying low."

"I've heard something to that effect." Dunn smiled at MacRae pleasantly. "That's why there's a cop sitting out in the hall now. The word's out that Steve intends to settle with you before he pulls out for good."

"What about this new lead on Corinne?"

Dunn flicked ashes off his cigar into an aluminum ash tray. "Forget it. We've lost enough money on the case and there's no possibility of collecting from Hockmiller."

MacRae didn't say anything.

"I said forget it!" A note of irritation crept into Dunn's voice. "What can you tell the police? That the Safety Director is hobnobbing with one of the Syndicate's men? That Corinne disappeared from his launch? How far do you think you'll get?"

MacRae continued to stare silently at the ceiling.

"Listen to me, MacRae," Dunn said in growing exasperation. "Use your head. Hockmiller is gunning for you, the Syndicate is certainly annoyed with you, and the police would like nothing better than to pin that killing on you."

"Bernie Benadotte?"

"Yes. I don't know how you manage to antagonize everybody—"

MacRae said, "It's a talent."

"You're a hard man to live with," Dunn said acidly,

"and that's a fact. But this is one time you're going to do the politic thing if it kills you. I got a wire from the head office yesterday—"

"New York?"

"Yes. They said to drop the Hockmiller case. We're going drop it, if I have to put you in a straightjacket. Is that clear?"

MacRae said, "You're the boss."

Dunn stared at him narrow-eyed, lips compressed in a tight line. "Anyway," he added dryly, "the doctor said that you'll be in here for two weeks at the very least. Which is something . . ."

MacRae let his eyes drift shut. When he opened them again, Dunn was gone and Margaret Ives was bending over him. He realized that he had gone off to sleep. He must have been doped pretty heavily.

"Hello, Maggie," he said. The grin hurt his face and he quickly let his features relax.

"Don't try to talk," she said in a funny voice and brushed his bruised cheeks with her fingertips. The light shining in back of her made a nimbus of her brown hair.

She sat down beside the bed, clasped his hand, and smiled at him with such obviously forced cheeriness that MacRae said, "What the hell are you looking so brave about? I'm the one who got beat up."

Startled, Ives regarded him with some confusion. Then she shook her head. "You're the most irritating man I ever knew."

MacRae gave a complacent chuckle and presently went back to sleep.

The barber finished shaving MacRae, who was propped up in bed, gathered his tools together and went out. MacRae ran his fingers over his chin.

"Damned butcher," he said.

Sergeant Emberger stood up. He had been sitting by the window and staring down at the quiet street below as he waited for the barber to leave the room. Moving over to the chair beside the bed, he sat down and glanced at a book which MacRae had been reading.

MacRae thumped the book in disgust. "According to all the stories you read, you'd think a private detective lived like a rooster in a hen house."

"I never read 'em," said Sergeant Emberger indifferently.

MacRae picked up the volume and hurled it fluttering out the open window. He regarded Emberger malevolently.

"I didn't write it," the sergeant said.

MacRae chose to ignore this. "These damn books were beginning to give me a complex," he said. "Maybe I was all wet. Maybe I'd been overlooking my opportunities. So this time I was on the lookout. I was on the make, see."

"Yeh," said Sergeant Emberger with growing interest. "What happened?"

"Nothing," said MacRae in disgust. "The only good-looking babe turns out to be a pushover: a semi-professional whore."

Emberger's eyes widened and he whistled soundlessly.

"The hell you say," he said. "I never would have guessed it. Why, she's pretty as a picture. What the hell are you griping about, you lucky son-of-a-gun!"

MacRae frowned. "Who do you think I'm talking about?"

"Why, that little brown-haired girl in your office.

What's her name? Ives? That's it, Margaret Ives."

"Ives!" MacRae roared. "Whatever gave you the idea I was talking about Ives? If I wasn't flat on my back, I'd—"

"O.K., O.K.," said the sergeant defensively. "I didn't mean anything by it. I was as surprised as you."

MacRae glared at him suspiciously. After an uncomfortable silence, he asked, "What did you come to see me about?"

"I wanted you to look at some pictures. See if you can make the other mug that beat you up. We picked out about a dozen from your description." He took a sheaf of official photographs from his pocket.

MacRae glanced through them. "That's him," he said at the third photograph.

"Pinky Hamilton. That's what they figured in I.B. He used to be a fighter. Heavyweight. The boxing commission kicked him out of the ring."

MacRae handed back the photographs. "What did the FBI find out about those slugs that killed Warren?"

The sergeant shot him an inquiring glance. "Dunn told us your agency had dropped the case."

"I keep forgetting," said MacRae dryly. "What about those slugs?"

Emberger hesitated. "This is on the q.t., you understand," he said finally, "but it was the same gun that killed Big Steve. That ain't all. We found a witness who saw Little Steve leave Warren's place just a short while before you found the body."

"Little Steve! So he was out there about the time Warren was shot. If there's anything I can do to help pin it on that bastard—"

"We'll get him," said Emberger.

"I hope he fries," said MacRae with utter sincerity.

MacRae was sitting in the chair by the window, smoking a cigarette and placidly reading the paper. His door was open and from the corridor outside came the rustle of starched uniforms, the whisper of rubber-soled shoes, the tinkle of crockery. A heading caught his eye:

GIRL WHO STROLLED NUDE GETS 30 DAYS AS TIPSY

Louisville, Ky. — Edith Earle, 26, who created a sensation yesterday when she appeared nude in the downtown area, was sentenced to 30 days in jail today.

"Goddamn!" said MacRae in amusement, "and I had to be stuck up here in this hospital!" His eyes skipped on down the page.

PRISONERS DRINK EVIDENCE

Louisville, Ky. — Complaints that Louisville prisoners "drank up part of the evidence" stored by Beverage Control agents in Jefferson County Jail have been corroborated by the jailer.

He chuckled, scratched his chest, and flipped his cigarette out the window.

He turned the pages, scanning them briefly, but on the back page an item suddenly made him sit bolt upright.

TRUSSED UP BODY OF WOMAN FOUND FLOATING IN RIVER

Cincinnati, O. — The trussed-up body of a dark-haired young woman was found lodged against a boat-harbor float at nearby Sweetwine today. Her forehead bore bruises that may have come from a beating.

Copper wire bad been used to tie the woman's ankles and legs together. Her arms were bound to her sides. Five lead plumber's molds, weighing 8 pounds each were suspended from her back. Additional weights apparently had broken loose from the victim's ankles while she was in the Ohio River.

The chief investigator for the sheriff's office described the victim as being about 28 years old, 5 feet 2, and weighing 130 pounds.

Medical authorities said the body had been in the water about six weeks.

MacRae read the article through again, his pale blue eyes bright and flat. Then he tore the news item out carefully and put it on the table. Going to the closet, he took out his clothes and began to dress.

CHAPTER 9

MacRae's first stop was his hotel where the clerk greeted him with surprise. He said that the windows in MacRae's room had been fixed, and everything would be found just as MacRae had left it.

The room was hot and dim and saturated with the musty smell peculiar to ancient rundown establishments of its kind. MacRae raised the blinds and opened a window. Then he sat down in the red imitation-leather chair to get back his strength. The unaccustomed exertion had left him shaky as a newborn kitten.

After a moment, he got up and changed his clothes. He found his revolver in the bureau drawer where the maid had put it when she had cleaned up. The holster, though, was gone for good, and he slipped the gun in his hip pocket.

At the newsstand in the lobby he bought a Cincinnati paper and took it into the restaurant with him. As he had suspected, it gave the finding of the woman's body a much larger play.

MacRae read:

Investigators are pursuing leads in Covington, Kentucky, as to the identity of the unidentified woman whose partly submerged body was found late yesterday caught against a float of the boat harbor.

The woman at first was described by Richard Webb, chief investigator for the sheriff, as being about 25 years old, 5 feet 1 and weighing 120. She was wearing a slip and underclothes.

Police, however, are investigating the possibility that the victim may have been an 18-year-old Covington girl missing since June 28. Identification through outward appearance was impossible. The body had been in the water approximately six weeks.

MacRae tore out the item and put it carefully in his inside coat pocket. Then he addressed himself to his meal.

Safety Director Coleman was not in his office at City Hall, and his secretary informed MacRae that he wasn't expected back.

MacRae looked up his address in the telephone book and scribbled it down on an old envelope. Then he got his car and drove out Market to Frankfort Avenue.

Henry Coleman's home was in the Crescent Hill section. It was a large, substantial three-story white frame house, set well back in a huge, tree-shaded lot. MacRae rang the bell. He had to ring it several times before he heard footsteps approaching.

The door was opened by a young woman with sun-streaked blonde hair cut short and curly. She was so deeply tanned that her eyes looked startlingly blue by contrast. She had a good figure, he noticed, although a little on the thin side. As she regarded MacRae, her inquiring expression vanished, to be replaced by a shocked look of disbelief.

"You *did* find me!" she said and tried to slam the door in his face.

MacRae, however, had his foot in the way. He had anticipated trouble, though nothing like this. He was nonplused and wondered if the young woman was entirely sound in the upper story. These aristocratic old families produced rather peculiar offshoots sometimes.

"The name's MacRae," he said soothingly, "from Gibbs & Stockpole. I'd like to see Mr. Coleman."

The woman stared at him dubiously. Then to MacRae's astonishment she began to laugh. She didn't sound hysterical exactly.

"You don't remember me," she said accusingly and opened the door. "I'm Mrs. Coleman. Betty Jean Coleman. The Venice bar. You bought me a drink and asked why I read murder mysteries. Lord, what a start you gave me!"

"Is that right?" said MacRae uneasily and tried to recall what he might have said. But he had only the foggiest memory of the incident. "I'm surprised that you remembered it."

"You're not an easy person to forget," she said in an amused voice as she ushered him into a long, wide, high-ceilinged entrance hall with parquetry floors. "I've been a little disappointed that you didn't look me up before—as you threatened. Just a moment, Mr. MacRae. I'll call my husband."

She started up the broad winding stair, sending him a smile over her shoulder. She was barelegged and the pale blue housedress certainly made the most of her figure. MacRae watched her hips move from side to side as she climbed the steps.

"Well, I'll be damned," he muttered under his breath.

She returned after a few minutes, telling him that her husband had suggested he wait in the study. "He'll be right down," she said and led him through the living room into a small room fixed up like an office.

There was an outside door, a big walnut executive's desk with a county map under glass, a cabinet that looked like it might disguise a portable bar, recessed bookshelves, a small corner fireplace with a model of a clipper ship on the mantel. The room was paneled in walnut with a low white calcimined ceiling.

She invited MacRae to sit down on the brown leather couch and sank into a low matching chair. She crossed her legs. They were long and brown up as far as MacRae could see, which was pretty far. His collar began to feel a little tight.

"Is Henry in another mess?" she asked brightly. But MacRae noticed her hands clenching the arms of the chair.

"I don't know," he said. "I'm after some information—that's all."

"Oh," she said and her relief was obvious. Her hands relaxed and the skin about her eyes crinkled in amusement.

"You know," she said quickly as if to forestall any questions, "I'm devoured by curiosity and it's all your fault. Why did you want to know why I read detective stories? I thought it was just a line at first. Then I began to wonder. Are you planning sort of a Kinsey report on murder-mystery addicts?"

"No," said MacRae, "it was just to satisfy my own curiosity."

"Don't you think it's a subconscious revolt against respectability?" she asked, uncrossing her legs and leaning forward.

"They're revolting all right," said MacRae, who was still feeling like the burned child.

"That's not precisely what I meant. A person can shuck off her inhibitions—vicariously, of course. Murder mysteries are an outlet for a whole lot of repressed desires that a person wouldn't dare give way to. Don't you think so?"

"Are you referring to anybody in particular?" he asked dryly.

"Yes," she said. "Me."

MacRae was a little startled by her emphaticness. He grinned at her amiably. "Who would you murder first? Your husband?"

Instead of taking offense as he'd half expected, she regarded him with an amused expression.

"I've been tempted," she admitted. "Henry can be trying at times. But I wasn't referring to anyone in particular. Not really. It's just that a person gets so fed up with—well—things, that they'd like to cut loose and raise hell generally. But they can't. And that's where detective stories come in. They're a release."

MacRae sensed an undercurrent of strain, of dead seriousness in the young woman's words despite her superficial jauntiness, and he wondered what could be causing it.

"A release from what?" he asked.

"Everything!"

"No," he said. "Something's bothering you. What is it?"

"A lot of things bother me, Mr. MacRae."

"For instance?" he said.

She laughed, then with sudden seriousness asked, "Why did you come to see Henry?"

"Business," said MacRae.

She gave him an exasperated look. "I'm not a complete fool," she said a little bitterly. "I—oh, damn! Here he comes now. Where can I get in touch with you?"

MacRae gave her his business card.

"It's been so interesting talking with you, Mr. MacRae," she said in an abrupt change of voice. "I had no idea a detective did so many fascinating things. Oh, here's my husband now."

MacRae looked around to see Coleman coming through the door. He was dressed casually in slacks and a sport shirt. He was a tall man tanned a deep suede and with slightly bloodshot eyes. His mouth was full but not slack, and he was growing bald. He exuded a faint aroma of Scotch Heather that MacRae figured probably came in a bottle. Obviously, he had been very good looking—still was, in a slightly decayed fashion.

Mrs. Coleman excused herself, and Henry Coleman shut the door firmly behind her and turned to MacRae.

"Sorry to keep you waiting, MacRae," he said and seated himself behind the desk. "What can I do for you?"

"It's about Corinne Hockmiller."

"Really?" The full red lips tightened. There was a faint glint of hostility, of contempt in his gray eyes. "I'm afraid you've put yourself to a great deal of useless bother, MacRae. You should have gone to the police department."

"No," MacRae interrupted, "not with this." He took the print of the sun bathers out of his pocket and slid it face up across the glass-topped desk.

Coleman looked at it without touching it.

"I see," he said at length. The contempt in his voice was unmistakable this time. "I see. How much do you want?"

Outside MacRae could hear a dog barking. A horn honked somewhere. Children's voices rose momentarily and died away.

"Information. I'm not trying to shake you down."

Coleman's mouth twisted unpleasantly. "And I'm not trying to bargain," he said. "I'm willing to meet your price if it isn't completely out of line."

"I don't think my price is out of line," said MacRae. "Have you seen this?"

He took the news item that he had torn from the

newspaper out of his pocket and slid it beside the photograph. Coleman read without comment.

"Are you laboring under the illusion that this unidentified woman could be Corinne?" he asked when he had finished.

MacRae didn't say anything.

"For your information," he went on with chilly amusement, "the police are investigating that possibility."

"Do they know," MacRae asked, "that Corinne disappeared from your launch while it was tied up at Cincinnati?"

Coleman's eyes suddenly narrowed.

"What are you implying, MacRae?" he demanded in a soft voice.

"Oh, come off your high horse," said MacRae impatiently.

He tapped the photograph. "By God, I can ruin you with this, Coleman, and I will unless you spill your guts right here and now."

Coleman continued to stare at him with a faint smile. "I hope you know what you're doing," he said.

"I'll worry about that."

"Very well, about three months ago, Corinne approached me at a party. She knew, of course, that I was fighting the gambling interests here in town, and she said that she had certain information that I would be interested in and suggested a meeting. I made an appointment with her on my launch."

"Was anyone else invited?"

"Yes. The other girl in this picture. Emily Franklin's her name, and a Mort Stevenson. Perhaps you know him?"

"No."

Coleman's lips thinned. "Stevenson," he said, "is a confidence man. He had me completely fooled, as I had been given to understand that he was a broker. Because of the very successful fight I have been waging against the handbooks, the Syndicate had sent him to try to ruin me politically. That picture is his work. It's one of a number of similar photographs which he took on the launch, and with which the syndicate attempted to blackmail me into laying off the handbooks. Fortunately, I was able to recover them without giving in to their demands. All of them, I thought at the time. However, it seems I missed one."

"How did you get them back?"

"I hired a private detective."

"Who?"

"Jake Youngblood."

"Where did you get his name?"

"From his uncle, the former city alderman."

MacRae ran his tongue over his teeth; his expression revealing nothing beyond interest.

"What about Corinne? What was her proposition?"

"She was a very frightened young woman," the Safety Director said dryly, "and with good reason. As you are no doubt aware, her husband had been murdered only a few months before. After his will was probated, it was learned that he had left the income from his estate to his wife until she died or remarried, when it was to revert to his nephew. You're familiar with all this, I assume?"

MacRae nodded.

"It was," Coleman went on, "an open invitation to this Little Steve to murder her. He had attempted to seize control of the handbooks following his uncle's death. In fact, it has been my opinion from the first that Little Steve killed his uncle."

"Yes," MacRae said impatiently. "Get along with it."

Coleman continued to regard MacRae with a polite smile as if he hadn't heard him. "Corinne," he said, "volunteered to supply me with certain inside information on the gambling rackets providing I would protect her from Little Steve. I agreed. She was able to tell me that Little Steve still had a pipeline into the police department, which enabled him to frustrate a percentage of our raids on the handbooks. Moreover, she knew the names of certain members of the force who were in his pay.

"From her husband, she had learned the details of a number of political tie-ups that would have been dynamite had we been able to get her before a sympathetic grand jury. Then there was that wildcat telephone network."

He shrugged.

"Unfortunately, she disappeared," he said, "before she could divulge any but the smallest fraction of what she knew."

The silence lasted a good thirty seconds. Then MacRae snorted. "Now," he said, "let's get down to facts."

"Those are the facts," Coleman said patiently.

"How many times did you see Corinne?"

"I'm sure I never kept count. A good many probably."

"And in all that time she never opened up. Why not?"

"She was very cautious. She wanted to be absolutely sure, not only that I would protect her, but that I could."

"Apparently she had some reason not to trust you entirely."

"What do you mean by that?"

"About that Cincinnati trip," said MacRae evenly. "Why did you have Kirt Crump aboard? The Syndicate's number one trouble shooter."

"MacRae," said Coleman pleasantly, "I don't find your insinuations very amusing. I've just about reached the limit of my patience."

MacRae leaned forward and tapped the clipping with a thick forefinger.

"Corinne Hockmiller disappeared from your launch that night. You've admitted that she knew too much for her own good. It must have been pretty easy to knock her out—the paper mentions bruises on her forehead—wire a few weights on her body, and dump her over the side."

Coleman laughed, not sarcastically. He seemed genuinely amused.

"I told you that we'd sent a couple of men to investigate the possibility that it was Corinne whom they fished out of the river. It wasn't. The body has been almost certainly identified as a Covington girl. It was not made public, but the autopsy revealed that she was three months pregnant."

He drummed impatiently on the desk top.

"I'm going to tell you exactly what happened that night so that you won't find it necessary to bother me again. Corinne ran out on the party. Mort Stevenson brought this Kirt Crump aboard. I didn't know he was a Syndicate man, but Corinne did. She thought that she'd been double-crossed and slipped ashore. I've never seen her since."

MacRae said, "Pretty neat."

"As it happens," said Coleman, "I have evidence that she was still alive after that night. At my suggestion, the police investigated the Cincinnati end. She returned to Louisville by air. Her name was on the passenger list and the stewardess identified her photograph. They were able to trace her to Standiford Field where she took a taxi. Then they lost her."

Coleman stood up. So did MacRae. The police work could be easily verified. He didn't think Coleman would lie about that.

So Corinne had been alive and in Louisville after her trip to Cincinnati. That was the important thing.

"May I have that picture?" Coleman asked in a cold voice.

"No," said MacRae bluntly. "And I've got the negative too—in a safe place. Remember that."

MacRae walked into the lobby of his hotel. He took one look at a slight, weather-beaten, sandy-haired man sitting in a chair reading the paper, and turned on his heel without stopping, and started back out. If he'd had any real hope of beating an unobserved retreat, it was instantly shattered. For the sandy-haired man looked over the top of his paper, said the one word, "Jaimie," not loudly, but in a tone that didn't even admit the possibility of being ignored.

MacRae stopped with his hand on the door. He grimaced like a small boy caught smoking cornsilk out behind the barn and turned around without any enthusiasm to face his brother.

"Why, hello Andy," he said in what he hoped was a pleasantly surprised voice. "I didn't see you!"

Andrew stood up and folded his paper carefully. There was a superficial resemblance between the brothers. They had the same sandy-red hair, the same uncomfortably cold pale blue eyes, but there the sameness stopped. Where MacRae was tall, burly with the bland, broad and battered face of a well-fed tomcat, his brother was a tough, stringy man who looked as if he had been put together with baling wire. He was a contractor worth conservatively something over a hundred thousand dollars, a pillar of the Presbyterian Church, and nominally the head of the family. An inflexible sense of duty had stamped itself on his seamed leathery features.

He said, "They phoned me from the hospital that you'd walked out. Twelve dollars a day for a private room! I don't blame you! Preying on sick people. You'll get just as good care at my place for four. You'd better pack a bag."

MacRae opened his mouth to protest.

Andrew glanced at his watch. "We'll have to hurry," he said shortly. "Helen will have supper waiting."

MacRae subsided. He was about ready to collapse anyway and in no condition to oppose Andrew, not that he thought it would have done much good. Andrew was about as flexible as a granite boulder.

Andrew never used his car to go to work but went back and forth on the bus because it was cheaper, so they drove out in MacRae's battered coupe. Helen met them at the door. She was a mild little woman, prematurely gray. She waited on her family, encouraged her husband persistently to dominate her, and always regarded MacRae with a breathless air of consternation.

Supper, as Andrew had foretold, was ready and by the time MacRae had come down from the guest room where he had been installed, it was on the table.

"Uncle Jaimie," Alf, the oldest boy, said.

"Yes?" said MacRae, wincing slightly.

"Uncle Jaimie, do you think Corinne Hockmiller was

murdered? Do you? We've been following it in the papers."

"I don't know," said MacRae, "but it looks pretty bad."

"Rubbish," said Andrew from the head of the table where he was cutting the steak into microscopically exact portions. "You may be a detective, Jaimie, but you're away off the mark if you think that woman is dead."

"Yeh?" said MacRae, nettled at Andrew's calm assurance. "What do you think has happened to her?"

"She's hiding out from Steve Hockmiller," he answered without the slightest hesitation.

"Where?"

Andrew said, "That's not a fair question, though I doubt if it would be too hard to locate her. The police, you, everybody has gone on the assumption that she's dead and conducted their investigations accordingly, when it's obvious that she's alive."

MacRae kept from grinding his teeth only by a strong effort. There were a number of things which it occurred to him to say, but he stifled them.

"What's so obvious about it?" he finally asked through his teeth.

"Of course, I only know what I read in the papers. But Steve Hockmiller is the only person with an adequate motive and if he had killed her, she would have been found. No, it's plain as the nose on your face that she's alive and bending every effort not to be found. Not that piece, Jaimie. It'll be tough. Take one by the bone."

MacRae deliberately took the tail piece and found it tough just an Andrew had said. He chewed viciously.

"Maybe somebody else had a motive you don't know about," he said sourly.

"I expect there are a number of motives," Andrew agreed complacently. "That's the trouble with the official mind. It tends to complicate things. I say get down to essentials, get to the hard core of things. It's too bad your agency has dropped the case. I expect that I could give you some pointers."

The disgusting part, MacRae thought irritably, was that he probably could. He ate the rest of the meal without appetite. The boys gulped their dessert, excused themselves and made a bee-line for the living room and the television set.

"Cheaper than the motion pictures," Andrew said calmly, as Helen poured fresh coffee and MacRae lit a cigarette. "I've been wanting to talk to you, Jaimie. It's about that young woman at your office. Miss Ives. I met her at the hospital, you know."

MacRae stared at his brother with a rather grim expression. "Did you?"

"A fine girl." Andrew's inflexible expression relaxed a trifle. He shook his head. "You're luckier than you deserve to be, Jaimie. Don't let her get away."

"What're you talking about?" MacRae demanded in surprise.

"Just that you're a bigger fool than I think you are if you don't marry her before she snaps out of her daze. Look at yourself—growing fat, bald and middle-aged. You must've aroused her maternal instinct."

MacRae glowered at him balefully.

Helen said in a fluttery voice, "Won't you have another cup of coffee, Jaimie?"

"No, thank you, Helen," he replied and excused himself on the plea of being exhausted after his first day out of the hospital.

"Think it over," said Andrew. "It's time somebody

jogged you out of your complacency."

MacRae heard him chuckle as he climbed the steps.

In his bedroom, he surveyed himself critically in the mirror above the dresser. He certainly wasn't getting any younger. But fat, bald and middle-aged . . . ?

"Goddamn him!" MacRae exploded violently.

MacRae had a mind like an alarm clock. He awoke promptly at one o'clock in the morning, rolled out of bed silently and dressed in the dark. Explanations with Andrew were a waste of breath. Holding his shoes in his hand, he tiptoed downstairs and let himself out the front door. He sat on the stoop to put on his shoes, then walked across the lawn to his car at the curb.

He was parked on a slight slope and crawling behind the wheel, he released the brake and allowed the car to roll down the grade. A half block away, he turned on the lights and started the motor and drove off.

Almost an hour later the moon was high and bright when MacRae turned in at the dark tunnel-like driveway leading to Monroe Springs. Cars were packed solid in the parking lot, but the attendant was nowhere in sight and the light was out in his booth. The shrilling of insects rose and fell monotonously, the frogs from the lake adding a bass accompaniment.

Superimposed on the natural nocturnal sounds of the country, was the brassy voice of the trumpet coming from the hotel. MacRae glanced at his watch. It was five minutes of two. He eased himself from behind the wheel, feeling a twinge from his taped side. He stood motionless, surveying the huge black mass of the building.

Here and there lighted windows looked down on

him like yellow eyes. A red neon sign above the entrance alternately flashed: DINE and DANCE. Down on the lake, mist drifted in luminous patches.

MacRae moved away from the car, walking silently but not stealthily. Reaching the building, he tried several dark windows, but they were all locked and he continued on. Reaching the rear entrance, he saw that the double doors were standing open. He glanced cautiously into the lobby.

Two couples, obviously rather the worse for drink, were arguing in loud tones about the floor show.

"I could do that!" one of the girls said with owlish gravity, then hiked up her skirt and rolled her hips. She teetered and almost fell, collapsing with a giggle into the arms of one of the men.

MacRae regarded them with distaste. There was no one else in sight. He slipped unobtrusively through the entrance and ducked into a dark doorway across from the ballroom from which flowed a subdued noise of dance music and voices.

His flashlight revealed that the room he was in was used as an office. Luckily, there was another door which opened onto a narrow uncarpeted hall. At the back of the hall, MacRae caught sight of a small service stair. He breathed easier once he had reached the second floor and made his way quickly to the employee's quarters in the wing.

The corridor was narrow and only dimly lit, as he remembered it from his encounter with Ward Bruton. There were five doors on each side. Bruton's was the third one down. Since he could see no light seeping from the crack under it, he guessed that the gambler must be downstairs at the crap table.

He heard voices in the main body of the hotel and

felt his palms begin to sweat. A girl's laughter reached him faintly and then he heard the sound of a shutting door. Then the silence closed around him again, broken only by the faint throb of the orchestra.

The first door on his left was locked, but it took him only a second to open with a skeleton key. Moonlight poured into the room, flooding it with a pale gray luminescence, revealing at a glance that it was unoccupied, unused. The second room was being used but the occupant was away. The fourth also. He searched them quickly. Sweat beaded his upper lip and temples, trickled annoyingly down his neck and sides. The upper floor of the old hotel was hot as a barn loft. He dried his palms on his handkerchief before fitting the key in the last door.

The bolt slid back with an oily "gluck." The door squeaked a little as it swung inward. MacRae paused on the threshold, his nose assailed by the combined feminine odors of scented powder, toilet water, and perfume. It was overpowering in the hot night air.

His eyes slowly circled the dark room. The window was open and moonlight projected a glowing rectangle across the rumpled white sheets of a bed. It had been moved directly beneath the sill for the sake of coolness.

MacRae stiffened like a pointer scenting a covey of bird.

A girl was lying on the bed. She was sleeping in the raw and the top sheet had been kicked against the footboard. In the moonlight, it was like looking at a photograph: all black and white and shades of gray.

She was on her back, her hair a dark shadow on the pillow. She looked small and rather thin; her flesh gleamed like polished silver. A pair of extremely high wedge-type sandals stood beside the bed. They must,

SWITCHEROO

MacRae realized, add at least three inches to her height.

He padded silently into the room, shut the door, and locked it. Then moving over to the bed, he bent down and stared into the girl's face.

At length he straightened, pulled the photograph of the sun bathers from his pocket and studied it by the aid of the tiny vest-pocket flashlight.

If it wasn't Corinne Hockmiller, it was her double!

And yet he was still puzzled. The resemblance was startling, but it was more like the resemblance between identical twins.

This was Mary Brown, the red-haired girl whom he'd dragged from beneath Bruton's bed, and it was Corinne too. It didn't make sense until he realized that unconsciously, he had formed a slightly erroneous but definite mental picture of Corinne from her photographs and description.

Despite the snapshot of her sun bathing, despite what Emily Franklin had told him about her losing weight, he had expected an older, maturer, plumper girl.

Extreme loss of weight, he knew, could do more to change a person's appearance than almost anything else. Corinne must have hennaed her hair and worn shoes with extreme heels to give her added height.

A clever disguise, he admitted grudgingly. Clever because of its simplicity.

He pulled the string, flooding the room with light. "Wake up, Corinne, he said. "Snap out of it!"

CHAPTER 10

The girl flinched, squinting against the rays of the unshaded electric bulb. "Is that you, Ward?" she began; then with a gasp she sat bolt upright. "Who are you? What are you doing here?" she demanded in panic.

"MacRae," he said. "We've met before." With a chuckle, he hauled up a chair and sat down with the backrest between his legs. Resting his elbows on the top, he contemplated the naked girl with considerable interest. He thought that she was pretty skinny and looked like a plucked chicken. Her breasts were small, almost immature, while the bones of her rib cage showed plainly through the skin.

Corinne looked suddenly disconcerted and whipped the sheet up to her chin. In the light, her hair was dark red. "What do you want?"

"You," he said. "Here the cops and I have been looking high and low for you and all the time you've been parading around in the open right under our noses."

The girl's gray-green eyes clouded in sudden acute terror. "You know who I am!"

MacRae nodded.

Her eyes were fastened on him with dreadful expectancy. "How did you find me?"

"I saw you. Remember? In fact, I hauled you out from under Bruton's bed. I didn't recognize you then because, frankly, I thought you were a plump little brunette and probably a dead one at that."

He grinned at her amiably.

"But—but how did you recognize me? I've lost so much weight. I don't look anything like I used to."

"To be honest," he said, "I had a picture of you taken after you'd grown skinny. But I didn't connect you with the redheaded girl at Monroe Springs because I was so sure you were dead. Then I discovered that you'd come back to Louisville from that Cincinnati trip after all. After that it was easy."

He stuck his forefinger at her white frightened face and waggled his thumb like a revolver. "A good many people had a good many reasons to knock you off," he went on cheerfully. "The Syndicate, for instance. But I figured that they would've sent one of their boys around to do the job. They wouldn't have bothered to hide the body."

Corinne shuddered violently.

"Then there was Little Steve. But he would want you found as soon as possible so he could get his hands on that half million bucks.

"I didn't think Bruton would knock you off—or Warren. They wouldn't be apt to kill the goose that was laying the gold eggs.

"No sir, you had to be alive."

Corinne was watching him with horrified fascination.

"But where?" MacRae said complacently. "And who was that red-haired dame hiding out at Warren's country place before he was murdered? Then I remembered the red-haired babe who was so chummy with Ward Bruton. The picture helped." He showed her the picture of herself and Emily Franklin sun bathing on Coleman's cruiser. "I'm going to keep this for my scrapbook," he added.

Desperately she continued to search his face for some clue to his intentions.

"Are you still working for Little Steve?"

MacRae's eyes suddenly glittered. "That bastard!"

Corinne nodded her head as if to herself. "I heard that he'd had you beaten. He tried to murder me." She hunched forward, holding the sheet under her chin.

"Please, Mr. MacRae, could you help me? He's still loose. And I—you see, I know he killed my husband—and Mr. Warren." She shivered, looking small and forlorn beneath the flimsy sheet. "It's been ghastly. I've lost over twenty pounds."

MacRae said cautiously, "What do you mean by, help you?"

"Couldn't I hire you as a bodyguard?"

"You could. If you have the money."

"Oh, I have the money. Lots of it."

MacRae glanced at his watch. It was two twenty-five. He wondered how long the crap game downstairs would last. He said, "You'd better tell me about it. You said that you knew Little Steve shot your husband."

She thrust out her lower lip. "Well, I don't exactly know that he killed Big Steve. But—but I've proof that he shot Mr. Warren. I was there when he did it."

MacRae concealed his astonishment with an effort. At length he said, "You actually saw Little Steve shoot Amiel Warren?"

"No, but I was in the house. Mr. Warren was hiding me out from Little Steve. He was the only person who had any reason to protect me." She shivered. "After I'd been there about ten days, Mr. Warren came home one afternoon and told me that you'd been hired by Little Steve to find me. While we were talking, Little Steve drove up. I got out of sight in a hurry. Steve was all steamed up about something. I could hear them shouting at each other in the library. I slipped into

SWITCHEROO

the dining room where I could hear what they were saying.

"Steve was sore because he thought Warren had double crossed him—"

"Had he?" MacRae asked.

"No-o," she said hesitantly. "I don't think so. But Steve was past reasoning with.

"Warren said something I couldn't understand and Steve began to curse him. It was dreadful. Right in the middle of it there was a shot!"

In her agitation she let the sheet drop far enough to expose one pink-tipped breast. MacRae began to have trouble following the thread of her story. He wiped the sweat off his face.

"It was too ghastly," Corinne said. "There was another shot. Steve rushed out of the library with a smoking gun in his hand." She shuddered at the memory. "He walked down the hall to the front door and went out. When I heard his car door slam, I ran into the front room and watched him drive off.

"I couldn't bring myself to go in the study. Then I thought maybe poor Mr. Warren was still alive. But when I saw him, I thought I was going to faint. His brains—" She bit her lips again. "They were all over the carpet. I was sick in the sink afterwards.

"Somehow I managed to pull myself together. I couldn't afford to be found there because it was just my word against Steve's. I went all over the house gathering up my things. It got dark before I had finished. Then I saw the headlights of a car turn in the drive. I thought I was trapped." She gave MacRae a wan smile. "But it was you and that girl. I heard you go around back, and I slipped out the front door. You had left your keys in the car. You can't imagine my relief."

MacRae glanced at his watch. "Go on," he said.

"There isn't much more to tell. I found a phone booth and called Ward and had him come get me. I've been hiding out here ever since."

"Why did you call Bruton?"

"I didn't have any other place to go," she said simply. "Steve was still loose."

"Why didn't you go to Bruton in the first place?"

"I thought I would be safer with Warren. My disguise was good enough to fool people who didn't know me very well, but out here there always was a chance I might run into someone. Of course it was pretty safe during the daytime. But the gambling crowd shows up at night and I've had to stay in my room every evening." She made a grimace. "It hasn't been much fun."

MacRae grunted and stood up. "Get dressed," he said abruptly. "You can give me the rest of the story on the way to town."

She gave him a startled glance, then meekly pushed back the sheet, swung her legs off the bed and stood up. With her back to him, she put on her brassiere, stepped into a pair of briefs, and dropped her slip over her head.

"Aren't you going to help me?" she asked, her voice quivering.

"I don't know," said MacRae. "That depends on Dunn."

"Who's he?"

"The manager."

"But you'll ask him to?"

"Maybe," said MacRae. "What happened at Cincinnati?"

"But the picture. You must know about that."

"Not your side of it."

She considered this with her head cocked to one side. At length, she picked up a comb, sat down on the edge of the bed, and began to comb her hair with reckless vicious strokes.

"But it doesn't really have anything to do with the other," she protested.

MacRae didn't say anything.

She shrugged helplessly. "When I learned the terms of the will, I was scared. I thought I would scrimp and save every penny I could get together. Then when I had enough, I would just go away. So I moved to the Tower Arms because it was so much cheaper."

She put down the comb and began to pull on her stockings.

"Twice I saw Little Steve hanging around outside. It sent me into a panic. I decided that I would go to the Safety Director and make a clean breast of everything I knew. I thought if I did, they would be able to put Little Steve out of business and maybe even send him to jail."

"Why the Safety Director?"

Her voice sounded contrite. "It's not very nice, but I'd heard that he was—that he liked the girls, you know, and—and he had been fighting the handbooks. And, well, I thought I could get him to listen to me."

"Did you?"

"Yes. I went to a few parties on his launch, and he promised to help me." As she talked, she fastened her stockings to her garters, put on shoes, stood up and pulled a dress over her head. Then she shook, plucked and wriggled everything into place. "A man by the name of Stevenson used to come along on the parties.

He was supposed to be a broker or something and upper crust. He was smooth all right, but I put him down as a high-class grifter.

"I didn't know it then, but the Syndicate had sent him down to get something that they could put pressure on Coleman with. They couldn't pull any rough stuff with him. And Coleman had been giving them a hard time."

She lit a cigarette. With her head bent slightly over the match's flame, her features looked delicate, almost childlike.

"Anyway, Mort took those pictures on the sly. Then, just before I cleared out, Little Steve tried to break into my apartment. I had a bolt on the kitchen door, but he tapped the glass and broke it. He didn't make much noise, but I hadn't gone to sleep. I screamed and managed to get out into the hall. My screams woke up the other tenants and Steve had to run for it.

"But it put me in a panic. I knew what he was up to. He wanted to kill me and make it look like it had been done by a burglar. A couple of houses in the neighborhood had been broken into by thieves, and at one place a woman had been raped. The cops would have laid the blame for my murder on them. I was a nervous wreck."

MacRae heard a car pull away from around front but he didn't interrupt.

"I went to see Coleman the next morning," she resumed. "He told me that he was taking a run up the river in his launch. He said we could make a party of it and I'd be perfectly safe aboard his boat and it would give us a couple of days to decide what was the best thing to do.

SWITCHEROO 159

"Mort came along and Emily. I didn't think anything was likely to happen with them aboard. But when we got to Cincinnati another couple joined us. It was Kirt Crump. He's sort of a fixer, a troubleshooter for the Syndicate. I thought I was going to die. I drank more than I should to buck up my courage. I can't hold liquor very well and I passed out.

"I don't know what happened after that for a while but I came to on a bunk in one of the cabins. I could hear voices. The walls were pretty thin. I could recognize Kirt Crump and Coleman. They seemed to be arguing. I'd made a lot of claims about what I knew when I was trying to get Coleman to help me. And I'd talked about Crump.

"Then I heard them mention my name and pictures. Coleman began to swear. I was petrified. After a while, they went out on deck again.

"I looked out my window. There wasn't anyone on that side of the boat and we were tied up to a pier. I crawled through the window and got away without being seen. I spent the night in a hotel and the next morning I flew back to Louisville. I called Warren, because with the Syndicate after me as well as Steve, I was half crazy with fear. He picked me up at the corner of Fourth and Broadway and took me out to his home."

She hadn't been looking at MacRae as she talked, but now she lifted her head and tried to read his expression.

"I don't know what I'll do," she said simply, "if you don't help me."

"O.K.," said MacRae. "I reckon Dunn will take it on. But it'll cost plenty just for a straight protection job."

To his consternation, she leaned forward, seized his

hand, pressed her cheek against it, while tears rolled slowly out of her eyes.

"I'm so grateful. I'm so grateful," she said.

MacRae took back his hand uncomfortably. "What the hell," he said, "you're paying for what you get. You'd better start packing."

She sprang eagerly to her feet. "I was so afraid you wouldn't help me." She pulled an overnight bag from beneath the bed and began to throw things into it.

MacRae watched her aloofly. She kept up an incessant chatter about what a relief it was to get everything off her chest. It was as if a weight had been lifted from her, she said. She wasn't afraid now that she had MacRae to stand between her and Little Steve. The police would catch him soon. She was sure of it. She might even go away herself to Florida or Canada for a vacation until he was safely behind bars.

She was bending over her bag to fasten it when they both heard footsteps approaching along the hall outside. Without straightening she glanced over her shoulder at MacRae, her face stricken. Her lips silently framed the single word, "Ward."

MacRae's eyes had gone flat and cold. He stepped quickly to the wall where the opening door would conceal him. The footsteps came closer, reached the door, and halted. Knuckles rapped at the panel.

"Wh-who is it?" Corinne called faintly.

"Ward," the gambler's voice replied. "Who did you think it was, baby?" The door knob turned. The door vibrated impatiently as he found it locked. "Open up."

"I'm too tired tonight," Corinne said in a frightened voice.

There was a loud uncomfortable silence. MacRae wiped his palm on his trouser leg and took the revolver

SWITCHEROO

out of his hip pocket.

Ward Bruton said, "What's the matter with you, baby?" The knob rattled again. "Come on, open the door."

She shot MacRae a frightened look. He nodded for her to unlock the door.

"Don't tear it down," she called, crossing the room on stiff legs and inserting the key.

The door opened violently and Ward Bruton strode in, pushing the girl aside. He was in shirt sleeves. A lock of his lank black hair hung down across his forehead and there were sooty rings under his eyes. He saw the overnight bag.

"So," he said softly, "you were going to run out on me, baby?"

Involuntarily Corinne's eyes flicked past him to MacRae. Bruton caught the glance and stiffened as if MacRae had jammed the revolver against his spine. With his arms held away from his sides, he turned slowly around.

Corinne licked her lips. Her skin was bloodless, giving it the translucent quality of wax.

"Hello, Bruton," MacRae said dryly. "Have a good night?"

"Penny ante," said the gambler.

MacRae jerked his head at Corinne. "Get your bag."

She was careful to cross behind Bruton as she took her suitcase from the bed and returned to the door. The gambler's eyes followed her. There was a small sardonic smile on his lips.

"Goodbye, baby," he said. "I'll be around to see you."

Daybreak wasn't far off when MacRae parked in the alley behind City Hall. The streets were silent and deserted. From the direction of Fifth Street a car door slammed and a motor burst into life, echoing hollowly between the dark buildings. He felt Corinne clutch nervously at his arm as they climbed the steps.

"You'll stick by me," she pleaded.

He nodded reassuringly. However, no sooner had he turned her over to the startled detective in charge than he excused himself and went to phone Dunn. He had to go into considerable detail with Isaac Dunn before the manager would agree to take the job. Finally he said that he would root out Feeny, the firm's legal adviser, and be right over.

MacRae hung up the phone. He was tired and he smoked a cigarette in the gloomy hall before going out to an all-night cafe where he got coffee in paper containers and brought one back to Corinne.

Colonel Hendricks, the chief of police, arrived shortly thereafter, then Major Bridwell and a man from the Commonwealth attorney's office.

Corinne had to tell her story over and over again.

MacRae threw a knee across a corner of a desk and listened placidly. The girl's story was essentially the same as she had told him except that she was careful not to mention either the Safety Director or the Cincinnati episode. She was very convincing.

The prosecutor's man was a nervous young fellow in shirt sleeves. He kept fidgeting around the room as the questioning proceeded. The air was layered with smoke. He stopped finally in front of Corinne and said, "There was a concealed wall safe in Warren's study. I don't suppose you knew about that?"

Corinne said quickly, "Oh, yes, but I do. Steve made Warren open it. He must've taken everything in it." She appeared prettily confused. "I looked," she confessed. "Amiel kept a large sum of cash there in case of an emergency, and I didn't have any money. I was afraid to go to my bank. But the money was gone."

MacRae raised his sandy eyebrows but didn't say anything.

Dunn arrived in the midst of the inquiry with Feeny and Walker in tow. The police were understandably annoyed that Corinne had hired a private agency to protect her. The story of her return was bound to create a sensation, MacRae knew, and the fact that she was afraid to trust herself to police protection would not look well.

The man from the Commonwealth attorney's office began insisting that Corinne be held as a material witness. They had the person who had seen Little Steve Hockmiller leaving Warren's house the afternoon of the murder, he admitted, but Corinne's testimony was the clincher.

MacRae left them to their legal wrangling and drew Sergeant Emberger aside. "What was that business about the safe?" he inquired. "Were those Corinne's fingerprints on it?"

Emberger swore. "Yes," he said.

MacRae said, "She didn't fall in the trap, eh?" and chuckled much to Emberger's disgust. His eyes felt as if they had sand under the lids and his head ached. He hung around for a few minutes longer, then told Dunn that he was practically out on his feet and left.

When he reached the street, he saw that it was broad daylight. In his room he barely had strength left to undress and flop on the sheets. He slept twenty-four hours like a dead man.

CHAPTER 11

MacRae woke feeling more like himself than at any time since the beating. He bawled a few verses of *You Two-Timed Me Once Too Often* as he stood under the shower. Even in the bathroom he didn't sound good. But since he was inclined to be suspicious of musical talent in men anyway, his own deficiency only served to reassure him.

When he reached the office he found it deserted except for Ives. She pushed her glasses up on her forehead and grinned at him fondly.

"We were beginning to wonder if you'd gone into hibernation," she said.

"Just when I've become famous!"

"So, you've been reading the papers."

"Yes," he admitted. "How did you like those headlines: 'Sleuth Locates Missing Girl'? And that sentence: 'Working on his own after all the official agencies had given her up for dead, MacRae found the frightened young widow hiding in a resort hotel, and thus by her testimony enabled the police to clear up two unsolved murders?' What about dinner tonight?"

She laughed and shook her head.

"Why not?" MacRae demanded in surprise.

"You're to relieve Walker tonight. Mr. Dunn has put a twenty-four-hour-a-day guard on Corinne until Steve is caught."

"The night shift, eh?" He began to grin lecherously. "Well, well," he said.

"Jaimie," she burst out in a distressed voice. "You

couldn't! You—you just couldn't!"

"Why not?"

She stared at him soberly. "I think you're horrible." She whirled suddenly, ran into Dunn's private office, and locked the door.

MacRae gazed after her with a bewildered expression. He crossed the office and laid his ear against the panel. He thought he could hear her sniffing.

"Maggie," he said, "open the door. I was only kidding."

"Go away," she said in a muffled voice.

"But Maggie," he said earnestly, "I wouldn't lay that dame—"

"O-oooo!" she wailed.

MacRae began to lose patience. He rattled the knob. "Open up," he said. "Goddamn it, I told you I was only kidding."

He heard a discreet cough behind him and wheeled around to meet Isaac Dunn's icy stare.

"Glad to see you're so much better," Dunn said.

MacRae could feel his face heat up like from an electric blanket.

"You can come out now, Miss Ives," Dunn said, raising his voice slightly. "I think that between the two of us we can restrain the beast in him."

There was a profound silence from Dunn's office, then the door opened slowly and Ives crept out. Her cheeks were scarlet. She gave the manager a brief, appalled glance, scooted across the reception room and out through the side door.

Dunn said, "I want to talk to you, MacRae."

Unhappily MacRae followed him inside. He sat down and put his hat on his knee.

Dunn said gently, "MacRae, your private life is your

own affair. But, by God, you're to quit trying to assault my secretary during office hours!"

MacRae opened his mouth and shut it again.

After a moment, Dunn said, "Do I make myself clear?"

"Yes."

"Very well," said Dunn. "Now then, about Corinne—"

"I never laid a hand on that bitch!" MacRae protested in an injured roar. "If she—"

Dunn stopped him with a gesture.

"I doubt if she'd complain if you did," he said dryly. "Her story is as full of holes as a sieve. You realize that, don't you?"

MacRae regarded Dunn with only slightly less animosity. "Of course she's lying," he said finally. "She couldn't have stayed at Monroe Springs without the Wheezer knowing it. That means Sam Jenkins probably knew where she was too."

"So?" said Dunn.

MacRae said, "By her own admission, she was out to get Little Steve. She had Coleman's ear. I don't think there's any doubt but that Corinne is hand and glove with the outfit that's trying to take over the booking racket."

Dunn looked out the window, his round little face expressionless as a billiard ball. Finally he said, "Do you think Little Steve shot Warren?"

"The police say so," MacRae replied coldly.

Dunn sighed. "You carry a grudge a long way," he said. Then with a shrug. "You're to relieve Walker at nine tonight."

MacRae nodded and stood up. He put his hat squarely on his head and left the office.

MacRae was reading the evening paper in his room. He glanced at the alarm clock on the dresser. It was seven-thirty and not quite dark outside. He returned to the news.

The paper's sob sister had done a heartrending piece called, *I Married A Racketeer*. It was the second of a series and began:

> Today I talked with pretty Corinne Hockmiller again and was shocked to find her so wan and hollow-cheeked. Her bodyguard, a grim-faced man, met me at the door with a drawn revolver and escorted me into the living room.
>
> There I found Corinne curled up on the studio couch. She greeted me with a forlorn smile and invited me graciously to sit down.
>
> As we chatted, I found it increasingly difficult to realize that this girl lay under the shadow of death. That a murderer, who had killed twice before, was still loose and bent on her destruction. But then as I led the conversation around to her life with Big Steve Hockmiller, the notorious gambler and racketeer, I sensed the terror that had haunted her from her wedding day.
>
> She grew deathly pale as she told about the fatal evening when she had returned home to find her husband riddled with bullets, lying in his own blood on the living room floor.
>
> "I was numb with shock," she said tremulously. "I stood in the doorway half fainting, unable to comprehend that it was my husband there on the floor.
>
> "He had always been so vital, so alive. A strong violent man. It was impossible to realize that he was dead.

"And I was suddenly stricken with remorse that I had been unable to love him. He had been so harsh, so cold, so suspicious that our brief married life had been a continuous fight. I had lived in constant terror of him and only that afternoon I had finally summoned the courage to see a lawyer about a divorce.

"I stumbled to the phone and called Mr. Warren, who was our legal adviser."

"Why didn't you call the police, Mrs. Hockmiller?" I asked the pale, sad-eyed girl.

"I didn't think to," she replied. "I didn't think at all. I was half crazy with fear."

"Did you suspect then that your husband had been murdered by his nephew?"

"No. Not until the police told me that he had been shot at close quarters by someone he obviously trusted. Then I knew. Little Steve was the only man in the world whom my husband trusted."

"But you didn't tell the police your suspicions?"

"No. I didn't dare. I knew that if I squealed, death would be my fate. The vengeance of the underworld!"

MacRae snorted in disgust and put down the paper. Of all the crap, he thought, and glanced at the clock again. It was eight o'clock.

He stood up, put his revolver in his hip pocket, set his hat squarely on his head, and let himself out.

Walker met him at the door of Corinne's apartment. "Any trouble?" MacRae asked.

"Yeh, staying awake," said Walker with a yawn. His

cuffs were turned up. He had loosened his tie and collar, and he needed a shave. He looked more like an accountant who has been working late on a set of books than a detective.

The room smelled of coffee and cigarette smoke. A couple of magazines were strewn on the studio couch. There was no sign of Corinne.

"How's our baby?" said MacRae.

"Chipper as a sparrow," Walker grumbled. "But I'm bushed. She went on a shopping spree today."

"Any callers?"

"Yes," Walker nodded. "A nice little dish from next door. Name of Emily Franklin. Then Sam Jenkins, the layoff man, dropped in this evening. They had a confab in the bedroom. There's some hot coffee on the stove if you want it."

"Sam Jenkins," MacRae said with a frown. "So Sam was here. You didn't happen to overhear what they were talking about?"

"No. They talked too low," Walker buttoned his collar, adjusted his tie, and put on his hat and coat. He went in the back hall and knocked on the bedroom door.

"I'm leaving, Mrs. Hockmiller," he said. "MacRae's here."

MacRae locked the door after Walker had gone. He wandered through the kitchen where he examined the open window. It looked out onto the back porch overhanging the alley. He shut and locked the window.

There was a sheer, three-story drop beneath the bedroom windows. Returning to the living room, he sat down on the couch and lit a cigarette.

There was a mystery on the end table. He began to experience that frustrating sense of inadequacy and annoyance as he started to skip through it.

Suddenly he heard Corinne give a whimpering cry from her bedroom.

"MacRae!" she shrieked. "Quick! Oh, God, hurry! In here!"

He dropped the book and sprang to his feet. But he pulled up short in the hall and sidled through the door of the bedroom cautiously. The room was empty except for Corinne, who didn't have on a stitch of clothes. She was flattened dramatically against the wall beside the window.

"Wow!" said MacRae, surprised but enthusiastic.

"Th-the street, you lunkhead!" Corinne's eyes were round with terror.

MacRae scowled. He figured his mistake had been a natural one. Indignantly, he switched off the lights. He felt his way across the bedroom to the window and drew the curtains aside. He found himself looking down into the dark side street. There was no light in the immediate vicinity and no traffic. Then a car turned in, its headlights briefly illuminating the figure of a man on the sidewalk.

The man was staring up at Corinne's window. When the headlights hit him, he turned and walked toward the mouth of the alley that ran behind the apartment house. A car was parked a little way down the street with its lights out. The man opened the door and climbed into the front seat and lit a cigarette.

By the flame of the match, MacRae could see another man in the car. They sat there, placidly smoking, making no move to drive away.

"D-do you see him?" Corinne quavered. "It's Little Steve! What will we do?"

"You ought to pull the blinds," MacRae said, "when you dress."

He jerked the blind down, switched the lights back on. To his further annoyance, he discovered that Corinne had slipped into a substantial green nylon housecoat.

"But it's Little Steve!" she cried, panic-stricken. Her hands fumbled nervously with the knot of the belt.

"You're letting your imagination run away with you," he said with a total lack of sympathy. "That fellow down there was from headquarters. There's two of them parked near the alley on the off chance that Steve makes a try for you. They're using you for bait."

"B-bait?" she said unsteadily.

"Don't get excited. It would take the riot squad to break in here now."

She expelled her breath with a relieved sigh. "I'm just being silly, I guess."

MacRae followed her into the living room, regarding her with a jaundiced eye. He was still sweltering from the uncalled-for rudeness with which she'd rebuked him a few moments ago. What the hell did she expect if she was going to flit around naked as a jaybird?

Corinne sank onto a chair and lit a cigarette with fingers that still trembled slightly.

"Corinne," he said suddenly, "why did you marry Big Steve?"

"I—I was in love with him," she said in surprise.

"Bosh."

"But I was," she insisted. "I was working in Amiel's law office. Steve was our best client. Whenever he came in, he seemed to fill the office. He was big and sort of brusque and—and exciting."

"But it didn't work out so well," MacRae prodded her.

She shook her head. "Not after we were married. I

was terrified of him. He was so brutal. He caught me flirting with Ward once. He knocked me down."

She pointed to one of her front teeth. "He knocked out a tooth and I had to have a false one put in."

"Where did you meet Bruton?"

She looked uncomfortable. "At Monroe Springs. Steve used to go out there occasionally to shoot craps."

MacRae leaned forward and said softly, "Why did you stay in Louisville after Big Steve was murdered? Why didn't you go away? Answer me before you have time to think up a lie!"

She sat up straight.

"I was saving up to go away," she said angrily.

"Rubbish!" said MacRae. "With the income from half a million dollars you could have lived like a duchess in Mexico. You could have taken a world cruise—"

"Stop it! Stop it!" she cried furiously.

MacRae said, "The truth is, you didn't have any money to get away because Warren was bleeding you white!"

Corinne's gray-green eyes blazed suddenly like the eyes of a cat. She sprang to her feet and went after him with a desperate insane fury: clawing, kicking, screaming. MacRae had never been so surprised in his life. He struggled to his feet and backed away, trying to fend her off. His heels caught in the carpet and he fell on his back with Corinne, on top of him, pummeling at his face, scratching at his eyes.

"Hey!" he roared. He lurched to his feet, got a grip in her hair.

She fastened her nails in his wrist. "Goddamn you!" she cried. "You nosey, pig-headed son-of-a-bitch!"

MacRae was desperate. He didn't dare turn her loose, and she was practically sawing his wrist in half. He began to drag her around the room by her hair.

The second trip around, she suddenly went limp.

He released her gingerly. She lay on the floor, her shoulders heaving with the violence of her sobs.

"Get up Corinne," he said.

She didn't move.

He stared down at her with a helpless expression. Sweat glistened on his forehead.

"Listen to me, Corinne," he said in a gentler voice. "You can't go on hiring bodyguards twenty-four hours a day. I don't know where you got the money you've been spending, but there can't be much more of it."

She said tearfully, "The newspaper gave me a thousand dollars for my life story."

"O.K.," he said, "but I've got to know what Warren had on you."

Her sobs increased suddenly in violence.

"Oh, Christ," said MacRae.

He went over to the mirror above the studio couch where he examined two long scratches on his chin. The noise of Corinne's crying grew slowly fainter and ended in a couple of sniffs. Pulling herself to her feet, she dropped into a chair.

"You've got quite a temper," he said.

"Th-there was another will," Corinne said shakily. "A later will."

"What?"

"Steve had Warren draw it up," she said, "after he found out about Ward and me. He left everything to Little Steve."

MacRae was staring at her curiously. Then he returned to the studio couch and sat down. She bit her lip, her chin trembled.

"You'd better tell me about it," he said softly.

"Why do you make me talk about it?"

He didn't say anything.

After a moment, she drew a shaky breath and said, "Steve found out about me and Ward. I don't know how he found out. But he went crazy. I'd never seen him like that before. He called me a tramp and other things. Horrible things. He said he would kill me but that I wasn't worth it and told me to get out.

"I was terrified. I went up to pack a bag. I could hear him moving around downstairs. He was drinking. I had just started to pack when I heard him coming up the stairs.

"I went into a panic, I guess. I ran down the back steps and out the kitchen door. I didn't have my bag, anything."

MacRae lit a cigarette. "Go on," he said.

She chewed at her lower lip. "I—I called Ward. He was furious when I told him and scared too. He said not to come to Monroe Springs. He told me to go to a hotel.

"I didn't know what to do. I decided I'd better go see Warren. It was about six o'clock when I got to his apartment.

"He told me that Steve had proof and had asked him to start divorce proceedings. He'd had Warren draw up a new will, too. He said I had a right to my things, though, and he'd take me out there to get them.

"I didn't want to go at first, but he insisted. He said he could handle Steve.

"When we got out there, nobody answered the door. I didn't have my key, but the door wasn't locked. We went in. We found Steve in the living room. He'd been shot."

"What about that new will?" MacRae asked.

"It—it was Warren's idea," she said in a faint voice. "He said nobody knew about it but him. He said he would destroy it and I would inherit everything.

"I—I knew it was wrong, but I was still Steve's wife. I had more right to it than Little Steve."

"Warren crossed you up," MacRae said.

She nodded miserably.

"He—he never did destroy the second will. He gave me thirty dollars a week and kept the rest for himself. He said I was lucky to get that. He could always find the second will, he said."

"Where did he keep the second will? In the safe?"

She shook her head.

"N-no. It was in his pocket when Little Steve shot him. I t-took it out of his pocket." She shut her eyes, sank back in the chair. The tears began to squeeze out through the long dark lashes again. "I wish I was dead. I wish I was dead."

After a while, MacRae said, "You've had a pretty rough time, kid. But if we can get Little Steve, you've nothing to worry about. The law doesn't let a person inherit from a man he's murdered. So you see the money's rightfully yours. You were still his wife."

She dried her eyes, staring at him with a look of pleased surprise. "Yes," she said as if talking to herself. "Yes, it is. Oh, Mr. MacRae, you don't know what a load you've taken off my mind."

"Don't forget Little Steve," he said dryly.

She sobered instantly.

"It's just a thought," she said, biting her lip. "I don't know if he's there, but he might be."

"Where?"

"He—he has a cousin living on Washington."

"What's his name?"

"Grossbeck. Albert Grossbeck. He's been careful to keep clear of the police, but he doesn't object to—to making a little easy money. He owns one of those big old rundown brick rooming houses. Little Steve could be holed up there."

MacRae didn't say anything.

"Does that help?" she asked. She had to repeat the question before he heard her.

"Maybe," he said. "At least it's worth a look."

CHAPTER 12

Major Bridwell came out of his office. He nodded at MacRae and said to Sergeant Emberger, "It's all set."

The sergeant got up hastily, wiped his hands and face with his handkerchief, belched unhappily. He had a nervous stomach, and the wieners and sauerkraut he'd had for supper in the restaurant across the alley weren't sitting too well.

"You got a gun, ain't you?" he asked MacRae in a tight voice.

MacRae nodded and heaved himself to his feet. After being relieved at Corinne's, he had returned to his room but he hadn't slept very well. It had been too hot for one thing, and late in the afternoon he had given up and had gone down to police headquarters to pass along the tip about Little Steve's cousin.

Because of the years he had spent on the force, they had consented reluctantly to let him accompany them on the raid. But they weren't happy about it. Which didn't move MacRae one way or the other.

He'd been sitting around the detectives' room, waiting patiently for the brass to work out the strategy.

Now it was ten minutes after nine, and outside it was dark and close with the electric feel of a storm brewing.

"Some people don't know when they're well off," Emberger said pointedly, as he led the way toward the rear entrance. His face was more flushed than usual and he kept brushing the holster at his hip, as if to assure himself that he hadn't forgotten his revolver.

MacRae didn't say anything. They went down the steps to the alley where a police sedan was waiting with a uniformed cop at the wheel. Major Bridwell climbed in back, breathing noisily.

MacRae squeezed himself in silently beside him. Emberger got in the front seat and, closing the door, began to talk immediately to the driver.

"I hope to hell this ain't a wild-goose chase," Major Bridwell grumbled. "I had tickets to the Amphitheatre tonight. My old lady gave me the devil when I told her I couldn't make it."

MacRae said morosely to the first statement, "I hope not."

Colonel Hendricks came out. He ran down the steps and got in another car. The two police vehicles moved out of the alley into the stream of traffic.

Major Bridwell said, "Don't use the siren," and with a sigh settled back against the cushion.

"Speaking of wives," said Emberger, turning around in the front seat so that he faced them, "I don't know whether to go home tonight or not."

"No?" said Major Bridwell, "why not?"

"There's a little blonde lives in the upstairs apartment," Emberger explained. "I've been chatting with her a good deal and my wife jumped all over me about it this morning. She was carrying on, crying.

Finally she said, 'Who do you like best, me or her?'

"'Honey,' I said, 'I don't know. I never had any of her yet.'"

The strain they were under made them laugh louder than they would have ordinarily. MacRae, though, gave no sign that he'd heard. He sat impassively, glancing out the window.

Emberger stared at him curiously. "Hell," he said finally. "I'd hate to have you down on me."

MacRae glanced at him incuriously. "Did you say something?"

"Nothing important." Emberger turned back to the front. They drove in silence.

When they reached Washington, the driver pulled into the curb and stopped before the darkened windows of a neighborhood grocery. A man detached himself from the shadows inside the doorway and identified himself.

"Where's the house?" Colonel Hendricks asked.

"It's about halfway down the block, Chief," the man said. "That big red brick house with the rooms-for-rent sign in the window."

"They're home?"

"I reckon so. Plenty of lights on. We got it plugged up tight as a rathole."

"What about the back?"

"There's sort of a coal shed at the alley," the man said. "We've got a man there where he can cover the back door."

MacRae asked abruptly, "How many doors?"

"Just the two," the man replied turning to MacRae in surprise. "Front and back."

MacRae looked at Colonel Hendricks. "I'll take the alley."

The colonel raised his eyebrows but didn't object. Turning on his heel, MacRae started down the quiet street.

It was a section of tall brick houses, of tiny grassless front yards, of milk bottles in window sills and dingy curtains or no curtains at all. A steamboat whistle moaned hoarsely from the river only a few blocks away.

A long time ago this had been a prosperous neighborhood inhabited by riverboat captains and such gentry, but the slums had engulfed it and the rundown old mansions were crawling with tenants.

At the alley the little clump of men separated. MacRae followed his guide into a black, evil-smelling tunnel: brick paved, lined with sheds. Something ripe squashed under his foot. A strong smell of outside latrines assailed his nose.

"Charlie," his guide called softly.

A man, stepping out of a dilapidated coal shed, said "Yes," in a high voice.

"The Chief's around front. They may flush him out this way any minute. Got your light?"

Charlie said, "Yeh."

MacRae felt his way through the coal shed and into a small back yard cluttered with junk. There were lights in the unscreened windows. Corners of beds were visible, rickety chests of drawers, lines with clothes drying. A small wooden back porch was tacked on at the kitchen door.

He leaned his back against the rough boards of the coal shed and waited. He could hear Charlie shifting uncomfortably within the shed. The noise of traffic was subdued and faraway.

The sound of angry voices reached him suddenly

from in front. He wiped his hand on his thighs, drew the revolver.

The voices stopped, then commenced again. He watched the back door patiently. The kitchen was dark and he couldn't see anything beyond the dirty pane of glass. There was a deep shadow on the porch cast by the house.

The door was halfway open before he realized it had moved. He brought up the revolver slowly. A man came into view, a tall angular man in his shirt sleeves, hatless.

MacRae pulled back the hammer with his thumb. The click sounded loud in the stillness. Behind him, he heard Charlie catch his breath. The beam of his flashlight lanced on, pinned the man on the back porch in a circle of light.

It was Little Steve Hockmiller.

With a stabbing movement, Steve fired his gun at the light. A heavy caliber. It boomed in the night like a cannon.

MacRae shot him. He aimed deliberately for the big easy target of Steve's body. With the same deliberateness, he pulled the trigger until the hammer clicked on the empty cylinder.

His first shot hurled Steve back against the door frame, where he was beginning to sag when the second shot smashed into his belly. The remaining three rounds hit him one after the other after he had crumpled to the floor. At each shot the body jerked as if someone had punched it viciously with a long pole.

Silence descended suddenly over the neighborhood as if everywhere everything had paused to listen. MacRae coughed, the acrid fumes of burned powder stinging his nose. Then somebody shouted from around in front, breaking the tension. There was the slap of running feet on bricks. A woman screamed. More yells.

MacRae crossed the yard to the back porch, Charlie was beside him with the flashlight. A big .45 Colt automatic lay at Steve's feet. It didn't take a coroner's verdict to see that he was dead.

Charlie muttered something and backed away. MacRae could hear him retching in the dark. He shivered suddenly as he stood on the porch waiting for the others to get there.

The alarm clock on the dresser said eleven-thirty when MacRae entered his room at the hotel. He looked tired and thoughtful. With a sigh, he divested himself of his coat, loosened his tie, took off his shoes and socks.

He eased himself down in the red imitation leather chair beside the window and closed his eyes. Instantly, the picture of Little Steve's body huddled on the rickety back porch formed behind his eyelids. He could see it jerk, hear the peculiar thud the .38 Special made when the slug smashed into meat.

He opened his eyes quickly, but the vision persisted. For a long moment he couldn't thrust it from his mind.

Disturbed, he set himself to cleaning and oiling the revolver, partly from force of habit but driven also by the need to keep himself occupied. He worked meticulously, finally wrapping the .38 in a rag and returning it to the dresser. He sat down again, picked up the evening paper although he'd read it earlier. But he couldn't keep his mind on the news.

At length he undressed, went into the bathroom, and turned on the shower.

When MacRae emerged from the bath, he donned a pair of gay maroon-striped pajamas and lit another cigarette. He selected a book from among three or four on the desk, sat down again in the easy chair. He got half way through the first chapter before he realized that he couldn't remember a thing he'd read.

With a scowl, he gave the book up and began to dress.

As he drove up he saw Ives had the porch light on. She must have been watching for him, because she opened the front door before he could get out of the car, and hurried down the walk.

"Jaimie," she said anxiously. "What's happened? You sounded so strange over the phone."

He said, "Let's drive around a little. I'm fidgety as a cat."

She shot him a worried, searching glance, then dropped her eyes and climbed obediently into the car.

"Has—has something gone wrong?" she asked as he pulled away from the curb.

MacRae said, "No."

He drove in silence out behind Jacob's Hill to the old Third Street Road with Ives watching him anxiously. At length, he circled around gradually back to Iroquois Park, drove up the winding hill road to the Lookout, and stopped.

The lights of Louisville were spread out beneath them in twinkling rows that merged away off into a bright haze. Five or six cars, their lights extinguished, were parked with their bumpers against the low stone guard wall.

He said abruptly, "We got Steve tonight."

There was something in his voice that told Ives what

had happened. She shivered.

"You—you killed him."

"Yes."

She was silent. He shifted in his seat so that he was facing her, but he couldn't see her expression in the dim glow from the dash light.

He said, "We trapped him in a rooming house. We were waiting for him when he tried to slip out the door. The cop put the light on him. He didn't have a chance."

She put her hand hesitatingly on his arm. "He was a killer," she said almost timidly. "He'd murdered his own uncle and that lawyer—"

"No," said MacRae, "he didn't kill either one of them."

"But the police—"

"I don't care what the police say. Steve didn't do it. He didn't trust Warren, but a man like that doesn't trust anybody. He can't." His voice was suddenly urgent with the necessity of convincing her. "Don't you see, Warren and the Hockmillers had their backs to the wall. Somebody was trying to ease them out. They couldn't afford the fight among themselves. Anyway, both Warren and Big Steve were killed with the same weapon—a .38 Special. Little Steve had a .45 automatic."

"But he could have got rid of the other gun," she protested.

MacRae shook his head. "Why hang on to it for six months after he'd murdered his uncle with it, then throw it away after he'd shot Warren? It doesn't make sense."

"Murderers aren't sensible people," she said desperately "They aren't sane or logical—"

He said, "Steve was a professional."

She sank back against the far side, staring at him through the darkness that didn't seem so dark any more.

"Besides," he went on inexorably, "Warren and Big Steve were killed by the same person. And Little Steve couldn't have shot Big Steve. He was at the Venice having dinner at his private table. A dozen people saw him. People in no way connected with him. Customers. Don't you think the police tried to break down his alibi? They worked for weeks on it."

A starter whirred in one of the parked automobiles. Headlights came on, described a swift circle as the car turned around. Ives' face, caught for an instant in the brief glare, looked white and strained.

At length she said in a faint voice, "You knew Steve wasn't the murderer when you shot him."

"I've known it for days."

"You deliberately killed him because—because of what he did to you. You kept quiet and let the police set a trap for him."

Her voice choked up and she couldn't go on.

"It's late. I'd better take you home," he said, and switched on the ignition, adding a little wryly: "It isn't fair to make you an accessory after the fact."

She reached forward shakily, as if to turn off the key, and let her hand fall.

"I don't know. I don't know, Jaimie," she said miserably. "It's so horrible. I'm all mixed up."

With his face slowly hardening, he started the car and drove back down the hill.

MacRae didn't show up at the office until noon the following day. He ambled into the reception room, grinned evilly at Ives, said "Hello, Maggie. Is Dunn in?"

She looked up with a start and said, "Y-yes." Her eyes were faintly red-rimmed as if she had been crying. She searched his face anxiously, but his grin was perfunctory.

"Is anybody with him?" he asked.

She shook her head. "Jaimie," she began faintly.

"Good," he said, "I want to talk to him."

He went into Dunn's private office and shut the door. Isaac Dunn was going over a report. Glancing up, he nodded at MacRae. He finished reading the paper and made several notes on the margin. At length, he pushed the paper aside and regarded MacRae impassively.

"You won't get any medals from me," he said.

MacRae ignored the remark. "I was talking to Mrs. Coleman this morning. She's worried about her husband."

"The Safety Director?"

MacRae nodded. "I made a few inquiries at my bank. Coleman has the reputation of being the worst deadbeat in town. He's been living on his connections and a big front for years. Lately, though, he's been loaded—"

"MacRae," Dunn interrupted icily, "I assume you didn't drop in just to gossip."

MacRae's eyes narrowed, but otherwise his expression never changed. "Are we still protecting Corinne Hockmiller?"

"No. I was talking to her on the phone a few minutes ago. She doesn't feel that she's in any danger since you were obliging enough to dispose of Little Steve." He paused, regarding MacRae with considerable interest.

"I wonder," he said, "how you will wriggle out of

having killed Little Steve if the real murderer happens to get himself caught."

"Resisting arrest," MacRae grunted and stood up. "I'd like to have the rest of the day off if you don't need me. I'm still a little shaky—"

"Sit down," said Dunn. "What did Mrs. Coleman want with you?"

A flicker of understanding passed between the two men, so brief that it was scarcely definable. There was no apparent change in their attitudes. MacRae said, "She wanted to find out how deeply her husband was involved in the gambling racket."

"What did you tell her?"

"Nothing. I asked her a question instead. I asked her if she knew a man by the name of Mort Stevenson. He was supposed to be a retired broker, I said, and was a personal friend of Coleman's."

"Did she know him?"

"Yes. She said that he came to the house occasionally." MacRae sat down again, put his hat on his knee.

"It's a funny thing," he said, "but I've never run into this Stevenson. I asked Mrs. Coleman what he looked like. She said he was a short blond man, a flashy dresser, good looking. She said he was quiet and his English was good except for occasional lapses. She thought he might have been connected with the ring at one time because his language was sprinkled with fight terms—"

"Sam Jenkins!" Dunn said.

"Of course it's Sam," MacRae agreed. "But I checked with Cincinnati just to be sure. They'd never heard of any Mort Stevenson who was connected with the Syndicate. There obviously wasn't any Mort

SWITCHEROO

Stevenson."

Dunn rubbed his nose with a thick fingertip. "You've been a regular ball of fire this morning," he said dryly. "But why would Sam go to all that trouble—"

"So the Syndicate wouldn't connect him with the Safety Director until he had the situation well in hand," MacRae cut in harshly. "So Little Steve wouldn't realize he had Coleman in his pocket until too late."

"Sounds reasonable," Dunn admitted.

"It couldn't be any other way," MacRae said sourly. "Sam's bound to've engineered the whole thing. Coleman was appointed through the influence of Youngblood, the former alderman. Sam got him under his thumb by a combination of ready cash and blackmail. Once he could make the Safety Director jump through hoops, he began to put pressure on the Hockmillers. Sam always was a boy with big ideas."

Dunn shook his head.

"I think you're right," he said. "But can you prove it?"

"I don't need to. When the person who killed Warren and Big Steve is caught, the whole dirty mess is going to blow up like a stink bomb." He'd been showing increased signs of impatience. He got to his feet again, set his hat squarely on his head. "That's why I've got to get to Corinne in a hurry. She knows too much. She won't last ten minutes with that pack of wolves if they get suspicious."

Dunn sighed. "Go ahead," he said reluctantly. "We've a certain moral responsibility in the case, I suppose. Besides, it would cast some reflection on us if it broke wrong. As it is, I'm liable to have New York on my back."

But MacRae was already striding through the door. In the outer office, Ives hastily put down her handkerchief. "Jaimie," she said miserably, "could I see you a moment? I—I was just going to lunch. I thought maybe you'd take—"

MacRae said not unkindly: "It'll have to wait, Maggie." But his eyes as they rested on her briefly were impersonal, remote. He didn't pause and crossed the reception room. The outer door closed softly behind him.

CHAPTER 13

Corinne opened the door of her apartment. She stared at MacRae in surprise and not a little dismay. She was wearing an old chenille housecoat which she was holding together tightly at the throat. Her hair was up in curlers and her face was devoid of make-up.

"It's Mr. MacRae," she said unhappily. "Oh dear, I'm a fright. I—"

MacRae said, "Don't let it throw you, baby. I don't mind." He ambled across the threshold so that Corinne had to get out of his path or be trampled underfoot. "Lock the door," he said.

She gave him a distressed glance. "Is—is something wrong?"

"Plenty."

She shot the bolt and followed him into the living room. MacRae, however, didn't stop there, but looked into the kitchen, the bathroom.

"There's nobody here," she said anxiously.

"I just like to be sure," he said. The bedroom door

was open. He glanced inside.

Several pieces of expensive new airplane luggage were on the floor half packed with clothes. The old suitcase she'd brought from Monroe Springs was open and empty. Clothes were draped over the back of chairs, the bed. A new olive swimming suit with built-in falsies, beach robe, slacks, a light coat, blouses, skirts. The top of the dresser was cluttered with cosmetics, and the room smelled of new clothes, scented powder, and toilet water.

"Well, well," he said amiably, "going away?"

"Yes."

"Permanently."

"I don't know. I hope so."

He said, "It's the first sensible thing you've done."

She appeared relieved at his approbation as if she had been half afraid that he might try to stop her. She went to the dresser, began to fold underthings, and place them in one of the bags.

A black traveling suit, a brassiere, slip, stockings, garter belt, and white nylon briefs were laid out carefully on the bed. Obviously, the clothes she intended to wear.

MacRae hung his hat on a bedpost. Clearing off a chair he sat down and ran his fingers through his sparse sandy hair.

"When are you leaving?" he asked.

"This evening."

"By plane?"

"Yes," she said. "The bank is handling my—my affairs for me. I'll have to come back later to settle everything. But I had to get away for a while."

He nodded sympathetically. "Where are you going?"

She hesitated. "Miami Beach," she said finally. "I've

got reservations at the Royal Palms."

He said, "Do they know at headquarters?"

"Yes." She sat down on the edge of the bed. "They said they didn't need me. The case is officially closed. I—" She bit her lip. "I've never thanked you for what you did. It was a brave thing to do—"

"Not very," he interrupted dryly. "It was more like potting a sitting bird."

"Oh, no!" she said. "He was a dangerous man. I've drawn the first easy breath in months—"

"Don't forget the Syndicate. They've a long arm."

Corinne went suddenly white. Her fingers began to shake. "I—" she said faintly, "I don't know what you mean."

"Quit stalling, Corinne," he told her in an amused voice. "You can't walk out on the Syndicate. You tried it once."

She licked her lips. "What do you want?" Her voice was a whisper. "What did you come here for?"

"To try to knock some sense into that flighty bird brain of yours," he said soothingly. "Baby, you're out of your class. Maybe you thought you were using Sam Jenkins and Coleman and Wheezer. But they were using you."

"No!" she said shakily. "No! That isn't true."

MacRae said, "You can't change anything by denying it. You're in a spot, kid. You can't help them anymore, but you're still dangerous to them. They can't afford to let you live."

She got to her feet, began to walk distractedly back and forth across the worn carpet. Her slippers made a slap-slapping sound. The yellow housecoat was fastened only with a belt. It split apart at each step to expose the inside of her leg. MacRae was aware suddenly that she was quite naked under the housecoat.

"What time does your plane leave?" he asked.

"Seven o'clock."

He said, "The only reason you need to worry about the Syndicate is because of Sam Jenkins and his outfit. They are the Syndicate here now, baby. With them out of the way, you wouldn't have anything to be afraid of. Hell," he went on persuasively, "you can't hurt the Syndicate—only Sam Jenkins and Wheezer and Coleman. You could blow them sky-high. The Syndicate wouldn't like it, but they wouldn't bother with you either as long as you kept clear of them. You could go away without being afraid to sleep, to go out after dark—"

"Oh, God!" she said in an agonized voice.

MacRae watched her, his eyes slightly narrowed. She came to a stop in front of her dressing table and sank down trembling on the padded stool.

"I can't," she said in a stifled voice. "I don't dare."

He brushed her objections aside. "Whose idea was it?" he asked. "Yours or Sam Jenkins?"

"M-mine, I guess," she said shakily. "But I—I knew Sam was ambitious. I knew he wanted control of the handbooks."

"Did you go to him direct?"

"No." Her voice was growing steadier. "No. I didn't do anything until Big Steve got suspicious about me and Ward. He was horribly jealous. He said he'd kill me if I ever two-timed him. I talked it over with Ward and persuaded him to go to Sam. I wanted to keep in the background."

MacRae nodded. "Sam like the idea, eh?"

"Yes," she said. "The Safety Director had just

resigned. Sam managed to get Henry Coleman appointed. They began to put pressure on the vice squad to close up the handbooks."

"What was your part in the deal?"

"I kept them posted about Big Steve." She hung her head. "It was a mean thing to do, but I was desperate. I was afraid to go on living with him and afraid to leave him."

"What did Big Steve do about it?"

"He fought back. When they took away phone service from the principal handbooks, he began to rig that wildcat telephone system. He was crazy mad because he was fighting in the dark. He didn't know who was responsible." She shivered.

MacRae said softly, "Big Steve was too tough for you, wasn't he? He had to be put out of the way, eh?"

She lifted her eyes. She looked a little dazed, like a mouse being played with by a cat.

"No, no, it wasn't that way at all. He overheard me talking with Ward on the phone. I didn't know he was even in the house. I was telling Ward that Big Steve had called Cincinnati for help. And I looked up and there he was standing in the hall. I screamed and dropped the receiver. 'Oh, God,' I cried, 'It's Steve!'

"He started after me. I ran out the back door and got away. I thought he knew everything. I took a room in a cheap hotel and tried to get in touch with Ward. But they told me at Monroe Springs that he'd just left without saying anything to anybody. Then I tried to get hold of Wheezer, but he was gone too.

"After a while, I began to calm down. I had to know what was happening. So finally I called Warren.

"He told me that Big Steve was going to divorce me and advised me not to contest it. He'd been out there that afternoon to draw up a new will. Big Steve had said I could go pick up my things. Warren said he'd take me out there."

MacRae said, "So Steve hadn't discovered what you were up to, after all."

She shook her head, catching a glimpse of herself in the dressing-table mirror. With a nervous air, she began to pluck out pins, taking down her red hair.

"He must have come in during the end of our conversation and heard me calling Ward 'honey' and telling him to be careful and how much I loved him." She bit her lip. "I don't think he even knew for certain who I was talking to. I tried to get hold of Ward again, but nobody knew where he was. I began to be afraid then. Really afraid. Ward had heard me scream and cry, 'Steve.'"

She stared at MacRae with a shudder. "You—you know what we found when we got out there."

MacRae glanced at his watch. It was only two o'clock. Sunlight poured through the net curtains, casting a ribbed pattern across a new overnight bag already packed and closed. It filtered across the clothes laid out on the cheap yellow spread. He offered her a cigarette, but she refused. He lit one for himself and puffed contentedly.

"Sam figured he was fixed with Big Steve dead, eh?" he prompted her.

"N-no," she said uncertainly. "Little Steve and Warren took over the organization and the Syndicate backed them up. Coleman got scared. He wanted to back down. I was worse off than before because Little Steve was trying to kill me."

"Yeh," said MacRae indifferently. "That's when Sam put on the pressure, I suppose."

She nodded. "Coleman had contacted Kirt Crump from the Syndicate. It looked like he was going to give in to them. Then Mort, I mean Sam, sprung those pictures on him. Coleman was furious in that quiet, nasty way of his. I thought he was going to kill me. That's why I ran out on the party at Cincinnati. I thought my number was up."

"Did Coleman know that Mort Stevenson was really Sam Jenkins?" MacRae asked.

Corinne caught her breath. "Yes," she said finally. "Sam was afraid that Little Steve or the Syndicate would smell a rat if they heard he was seeing Coleman. He went to a lot of trouble to fool them. We all knew who he was really. But I don't think Steve ever guessed."

She got to her feet and began to pack the rest of her things.

"What did you do then?" MacRae asked.

"Sam told me to get Warren to hide me out. He and Little Steve hadn't guessed the truth. Sam said I could keep my eye on Warren that way. He said if I would disappear, it would throw so much limelight on me that Little Steve wouldn't dare do anything to me. You know what happened. Steve killed Warren."

With her head bent over the bag, she closed and locked it. "That was the final straw," she said faintly. "I'd helped Sam get control of the handbooks but I wasn't any better off. I insisted they hide me until Little Steve was caught. Then you found me."

MacRae waited until she had closed the second bag. Then said coldly, "Most of that, I suppose, is true. It fits, anyway. But there wasn't any new will. That wasn't the hold Warren had on you."

Corinne's head jerked up. She stared at him in panic,

rising uncertainly from her knees.

"I don't know what you mean," she said so faintly he had to lean forward to hear her.

He said, "That business about Warren blackmailing you with a later will is nothing but crap. He was the administrator of the estate, but the income came to you. You had to turn it into cash and give it to him. He was as deeply involved as you. You could have held out for more than any measly thirty dollars a week. He wouldn't have dared expose you."

Corinne swayed, closed her eyes.

"The truth is," he said bluntly, "you killed Big Steve. You murdered your husband because he caught you phoning information to Ward Bruton. That was the hold he had over you. That's what he was using to bleed you white!"

Corinne began to shake. Her knees trembled. Her teeth chattered as if she had a chill. "I didn't!" she managed to get out. "You've no proof!"

MacRae heaved himself to his feet, laughed mirthlessly. "Of course I have. The same person who killed Warren shot Big Steve. And you killed Warren. You killed them both!"

"Little Steve—" she gasped.

"Little Steve couldn't have killed his uncle," he cut her off. "It's a physical impossibility for a person to be in two places at one time. He was eating dinner at the Venice when his uncle was shot." He advanced on her inexorably. "So he couldn't have shot Warren either. It's simple. You did it. You were the only other person in the house. If Steve didn't kill Warren, you must have. By your own testimony."

She was backing away from him in terror. Suddenly her heels hit the overnight bag. She lost her balance and sat down heavily on the floor.

"You can't prove it!" she repeated over and over between gasps. "You can't prove it."

"Shut up!" MacRae said brutally. "Of course it can be proved. You're a bungler, an amateur. A cold-blooded, vicious little amateur. I'd give ten-to-one the money from Warren's safe is in that overnight case."

He stooped for the bag.

Snatching it up desperately, Corinne opened it with fumbling fingers. Package upon package of green currency met his eyes. Her hand snaked in amongst the bills.

"Take it," she cried wildly. "All yours. There's still over twenty thousand dollars left. Take it. Take it! Only leave me alone. Go away and leave me alone!"

Her hand suddenly reappeared, dragging from the sheaves of currency a shiny chromium-plated revolver. Her expression hardened.

She began to catch her breath in dry, hysterical sobs. Her bare legs stuck out from the housecoat like the legs of a doll.

MacRae said, "Ha!" sourly and kicked the revolver out of her hand. He walked over and picked it up.

"Well, well," he said amiably. "A .38. This is the gun you used on Big Steve and Warren, isn't it? By God, that wraps it up."

Corinne closed her eyes and toppled slowly sideways. Stooping over her with a certain caution, MacRae turned up her eyelids. The faint was genuine, he saw. He shrugged, went out into the hall, and dialed police headquarters. After a moment he got Sergeant Emberger on the line.

"This is MacRae," he said. "I'm at the Hockmiller woman's apartment in the Tower Arms. You'd better get yourself over here in a hurry."

He listened to Emberger asking profanely what it was all about.

"Bring a stenographer," MacRae cut in, "and ask your questions here."

He hung up and went back into the bedroom where he settled himself patiently to wait for Corinne to revive.

MacRae was alone at a wall table in Jessup's, a coffee shop across the street from the offices of Gibbs & Stackpole. The coffee was lousy but only a nickel was charged for it and MacRae patronized the place doggedly.

Somebody said, "Hi," in a small voice and sat down across the table from him. MacRae glanced up in surprise. It was Ives. Caught off balance for an instant he stared at her, his eyes cloudy.

She said, "I was waiting for you to come back to the office. Mr. Dunn said I might find you here."

"Why, what is it, Maggie?" he asked in astonishment.

Her head bent a little. She was wearing a light blue summer frock. MacRae thought she looked so pretty that he wanted to kick himself for having told her about Steve.

She raised her head, stared him straight in the eye. "You're a lousy detective, Jaimie."

MacRae swallowed.

"You weren't fair last night," she said defiantly. "You've no right to—to spring something like that on a person and expect them to just sort of take it in their stride. I'm not one of those nonchalant creatures, you've been reading about. I'm just a normal person. You read too many of those books."

MacRae began to get red. "Now, Maggie—"

"Oh yes, you do! I've noticed. Here I've been following you around like an idiot, stumbling on a murder and getting sun burned and shot at. What do I have to do to convince you—slither out of my clothes here in the coffee shop?"

Ives looked so intense that MacRae got hastily to his feet.

"Not here!" he said. Then he began to grin. "That's not my style either," he admitted. "We need a license for the sort of thing you're talking about or I wouldn't be comfortable. Come on, Maggie, City Hall doesn't close for an hour yet."

THE END

Robert Emmett McDowell was born April 5, 1914, in Sentinel, Oklahoma. The family soon moved to Louisville, Kentucky, where he remained for the rest of his life. McDowell served in the Merchant Marines during WWII where he began his writing career in the pulp magazines as Emmett McDowell. He wrote stories for *Amazing Stories, Astounding Science Fiction, Planet Stories, Jungle Stories* and other genre magazines. In 1949 he began to shift over to detective magazines, switching to novels for Ace Books in the 1950s. In the 1950s McDowell became increasing interested in Kentucky history, and turned to writing historical fiction. He wrote one more mystery in 1965, *The Hound's Tooth*, as Robert McDowell. He died in Louisville on March 29, 1975.

Made in the USA
Monee, IL
24 April 2025